City Of A

Thousand Tears

A Beauty From Ashes Side Story

Story

Pamela Hart

PotatoChip
Publishing

Potato Chip Publishing

ISBN: 979-8-9888819-0-2 (paperback)

ISBN: 979-8-9888819-1-9 (e-book)

Also By Pamela Hart

Beauty from Ashes
Beauty from Embers

Dedicated to James L. Rubart and Thomas Umstattd Jr. Thank you for teaching me to use my wings.

A Strange Encounter

ELLIO FOUND A LOT of interesting things poking around dumpsters in the Downs, but this was the first time he'd found a foot. Peeking out from under the bin, the glossy black nail polish shimmered from the light of a distant streetlamp. Getting over his initial shock, the young man breathed a sigh of relief when his further investigation revealed that the foot was still attached to a leg. A rather shapely woman's leg swathed in black biomesh with metal grommets tracing up the seam from calf to thigh.

Falling to his knees, he ignored the water from the puddle now seeping into his jumpsuit and the cold rain that dripped down the back of his neck. He pushed his goggles up into his dark-blue hair. Another, older set dangled from his throat as he leaned down. Ellio peered under the dumpster and was further consoled that the shapely leg was still attached to not only a torso but an entire woman's body. She seemed to be all in one piece. Choppy black bangs fell in front of her eyes. Her face was flushed and smudged with dirt. Ragged gasps shuddered through her, breath puffing out as little clouds in the chill air. At least she was still breathing. Bodies sometimes turned up in the Downs, but not as often as one might expect.

What on Elorah had happened to her?

Ellio began to retrace the day's events in his mind. Had anything unusual happened? It was always smoggy and damp in this part of the city, but today's drizzle had been marked by a heaviness in the air. Like a static charge was building. Once the sun had slipped below the horizon and neon signs flickered to life, the air was split apart by a sudden downpour of precipitation. Water dribbled from two spots in the ceiling of his shop, circled by concentric rings of brown, a memoir of rainy seasons past. Ellio had placed a metal pot under one and a small blue bin under the other. The bin was starting to sprout some kind of orange mold. One of these days he'd get around to bleaching it.

With the poor drainage system in the Downs, water collected in the pockmarked streets. Puddles glimmered, made iridescent by the oil that dripped from leaky vehicles. Scraps of paper littering the alleyways dissolved into gooey blobs that stuck to the soles of shoes. The rain made everything smell worse—as if it sharpened the stench of rot and human body odor rather than cleansing it.

Just another day in the Downs.

After tuning up a hoverchair, replacing the carbolic intakes on a voltsleigh and fiddling with the exhaust manifold of a sling loader T40-B, Ellio had washed his face and headed next door to Roscoe's for a bowl of noodles.

Roscoe was a surly old goat. His noodles were soggy and oversalted—a failed attempt to hide the lack of other ingredients. But he was alone, like Ellio, and it was better company than huddling over the Zenon burner in his garage, defrosting a block of protein sludge that tasted like ergon gas. That got old *real* fast. Maybe he could afford one of those Avathysian ventilators one day. Ellio dismissed that dream quickly. Why waste time wishing for the impossible?

Another point in Roscoe's favor was an old gridscreen he'd nicked from a punter while playing slow-draw one night. The screen was a little fuzzy and emitted strange crackly sounds from time to time. But whenever Ellio went over, Roscoe would always put on the Retiarius matches. The female fighters' guild was Beulah's pride and joy, uniting people from the Downs and the wealthier districts of the city with a common interest. Even Aurea, the golden district, couldn't get enough of the violent arena matches.

Sometimes Ellio wondered what Aurea was like. Could the people living there choose where they worked? Did they even have to work at all? Or was every day a parade of unending delights like the gridscreen promos suggested?

It's gotta be better than this.

Ellio grunted as a cold raindrop slipped inside his collar, drawing him back to the present. Maybe he needed a hobby. People with hobbies were swish. They didn't muck around in the garbage after chicks who were drunk, or drugged, or possibly both. Bet people in Aurea didn't find girls in their trash.

The young woman shivered.

Ellio frowned. "Hey, you all right?" He shook her leg gently.

The biomesh cloth of her pants alone was probably worth more than he made in a month. He cringed at the thought of getting grease on them, but then again, the young woman was passed out under a dumpster. Clearly, she had bigger problems. But just to be sure, he wiped his hands along the thighs of his coveralls a few times.

"Hey, c'mon." Ellio craned his neck underneath the dumpster to see her better. "You can't stay here." He gripped her leg more firmly and tugged. The woman's head lolled back and forth limply; her eyelids fluttered but remained closed.

After getting no response, Ellio partially crawled beneath the rusty trash receptacle. "'Scuse me, lady," he whispered, sliding his hands lightly underneath her torso and dragging her out from under her makeshift shelter. He was careful not to let her bump her head on the way out.

Ellio kept his hands to respectable areas, but a blush still crept up his neck as he cradled the young woman against his chest. She looked about his age, maybe a year younger. Ellio had just turned seventeen a few weeks back. He couldn't help noticing she was beautiful, with full pink lips and a cute little nose smattered with freckles. She had golden eyeshadow like wings around her eyes. Ellio swallowed. Brushing her bangs back from her face, he held a calloused hand against her forehead.

"You're burning up!"

Groaning, he stood, carrying the woman. She was heavier than she looked. Dense little thing. How much did women weigh, anyway? It's not like he'd ever carted one around before. Still, she needed to get out of the rain.

Ellio staggered with the soggy bundle in his arms. Luckily, his shop was just around the corner, right next to Roscoe's Noodle Bar. He'd been taking out the old man's trash for a free bowl of beef broth when he stumbled into this whole mess.

Shifting her weight, Ellio stopped underneath a patched yellow awning that declared "Aubri & Son." He kicked open the door. Dust and metal shavings billowed in little swirls, illuminated by the grimy streetlamp.

Ellio shuffled through his shop, stubbing his toe on an axle that extended out from the work bay. Biting back a shout of pain, Ellio groaned loudly. At last, he reached the cot at the other end of the room and slid his newfound burden onto it. The cot creaked under the weight but didn't collapse.

As he set her down, the woman let out a soft moan. Ellio froze, watching her with wide eyes. But she remained unconscious, her breathing hitched and unsteady. Convinced that she wasn't about to wake up, he turned and rummaged through his drawers to find a clean rag. After running it under his rusty faucet, he draped it across her forehead.

Ellio watched her for a moment, his jaw tense. She appeared paler than she had a moment ago. And was it just him, or did her skin now have a tinge of blue? She must be freezing. Digging out a clean towel, he wheeled a three-legged stool next to the cot and hesitated. Her clothing was soaked, but the thought of changing it caused his mind to seize like an engine without oil. Nope, that wasn't an option. But maybe he could help it dry?

Sheepishly, he patted at the shoulder of her jacket, running the towel down her arm. This garnered no response from the young woman, but it did absorb some of the water. Ellio brushed the towel along her leg and dabbed at her bare feet. They were splattered with mud, and he found himself immersed in cleaning them for a few minutes.

In a way, it reminded him of his work taking apart engines and repairing them. His father had taught him the basics, but when Ellio began working on machines, it was like something clicked in his subconscious. Cables, circuits, nuts, and bolts—it all fit together perfectly in his mind—a soundless symphony playing just for him. When people asked him to explain how he fixed things, Ellio often had trouble finding the words. How did he make a thirty-year-old engine run smooth? Or stop a carbolic intake from kicking? He just knew.

The woman sighed again and rolled onto her side, disrupting his concentration. The movement displaced the rag, causing it to slide off her forehead. Ellio wheeled back toward her head. At least she was out of the torrential rain, but she remained unconscious, breathing ragged.

Further emboldened, Ellio took the rag and tried to brush some of the grime off her left cheek. He noticed a reddish patch on the side of her neck. It looked like a rash, the skin inflamed with little raised bumps. Ellio leaned over to have a closer look. As his shadow fell across her face, the young woman's eyes snapped open. They were such a brilliant violet hue that Ellio didn't notice her hand snake up until it seized his wrist in a bone-crunching grip.

"Don't *touch* me," she growled.

Ellio was so startled, he dropped the rag with a shout. "Ah sorry... Miss?" How should he address her? Her clothes spoke of wealth and social strata far beyond him. But he'd found her in the Downs, under a dumpster, for Dral's sake.

She still hadn't released his arm. Her eyes glared daggers at him.

Ellio felt like he'd grabbed a tiger by the tail. He could see his reflection shining in her fierce gaze. "You passed out," he stammered. "It was raining. I couldn't just leave you outside."

She flung his arm away with a sneer. "You can drop the Samaritan act." Grunting, she pulled herself into a sitting position. Then, taking a deep breath through her nose, she jerked herself up. She rose on wobbly legs and Ellio moved to support her.

"I said *don't*." She shoved him away. "I'm fine. I need to get back."

She grabbed onto the workbench to her left, using it to pull herself toward the door.

Ellio watched her struggle, but a latent survival instinct warned him not to interfere. He had an unnerving hunch that she would sock him in the jaw if he approached.

When she reached the end of the bench, the woman staggered a few steps toward the garage doorway. He could tell she was dizzy by the way she swayed. Too late, she sensed the inevitable, that she was going to fall. She reached out for his tool chest, but the wheels he'd rigged beneath it made it a poor support. She crashed to the floor, sending wrenches, bolts, and pliers scattering in every direction.

Ellio waited one breath, then two. The last thing he wanted was a fight with some strange rich chick. She struggled to rise three times before curling on her side, clutching her stomach.

Ellio knelt beside her. "Please. Let me help you."

She didn't respond at first. Her eyes were squeezed shut, lips pressed in a thin line. Then she gave a reluctant nod.

"I'm going to pick you up, okay?"

The woman cinched her arms around her stomach. Ellio could see her hands trembling, black nails digging into the fabric of her jacket like claws. He laid her on the cot and draped a blanket over her. She didn't look good. Her breathing was more labored, and her shivering was violent. He could hear her teeth chattering.

Ellio racked his brain.

Think!

She needed serious help. But who could he ask? There was only one person he could think of.

Ellio rushed back out into the pouring rain and sprinted to Roscoe's door, banging on it wildly.

"What's all that racket? Can't you people leave an old man in peace?" Roscoe stumped to the entrance and glared out, rheumy eyes blinking.

"Sorry! Sorry!" Ellio waved his hands apologetically. "It's an emergency, Roscoe."

"Emergency, my foot! You hyperbolizin' little miscreant."

"I'm serious, Roscoe. I need you to come to my shop right now."

The old man blustered for a moment more, but grabbed his coat. "Better be worth movin' these aching bones or I'm gonna clout you one," he mumbled under his breath. When he laid eyes on the swanky Aurean shivering on Ellio's cot, he raised his brows.

"It's not like that," Ellio insisted, rolling his eyes. "I noticed her holed up under the dumpster when I went to take out the trash. She's sick, feverish. I don't know how to help her."

"Aurea got access to doctors and the like."

"But she doesn't have any ID. And I doubt those doctors would do a house call in the Downs."

Roscoe stumped around the shop for a minute, thinking. Eyeing the bolts and tools still strewn around the floor, he turned back to Ellio. "She do all this?"

"For the split second she could stay conscious."

"Got spirit, don't she?"

Remembering her fiery glare, Ellio shrugged. "That's one way to put it."

Roscoe's face brightened and he flashed a toothy grin. "I have somethin' might do the trick. An Eirenian atomizer."

"How'd you score one of those?"

"Got it off a trader a while back."

"Lifted it, you mean."

Roscoe didn't deny it. Instead, he walked to the edge of the garage and peered into the pouring rain from under the safety of the awning. "Kept tellin' myself I was savin' it for a rainy day."

Ellio didn't say anything. An Eirenian atomizer was worth a fortune. They were rumored to cure all kinds of ailments. But with the hostility between Eiren and Gehenna, those kinds of meds were almost impossible to come by nowadays. And Roscoe wasn't getting any younger. This lady appeared to be from the Aurea district, but there was no guarantee she'd repay them.

"I can't ask you to give that up, Roscoe."

"You didn't," the old man grunted, but there was a warmth underneath it. He shuffled back to his shop and returned with a small glass vial a few minutes later. The atomizer resembled a syringe, with a plastic cone on the end. The liquid inside was a brilliant emerald green.

"How does it work?" Ellio asked.

"We're supposed to stick it in her nose." Roscoe rubbed a hand over his balding head.

"Her nose?" Ellio asked incredulously. "That doesn't sound right."

"Look, kid, you asked me for help. This is what I got. Atomizers are designed for sick, weak people, possibly unconscious. Like your lady friend here. You're lucky it isn't a pill she'd have to swallow."

Ellio threw up his hands. "Fine, whatever you say."

Roscoe held the atomizer out to him. "You put it in her nose and press down till all the liquid is gone. She's gotta breathe it all in, you hear?"

"Okay, stick the plastic cone in her nose. Make sure she breathes it all." Ellio took the atomizer and held it under the light. The green liquid glittered inside.

"Please work," he whispered, slipping the atomizer in her nostril, and pressing down on the plunger.

Her arms shot up, grabbing at him, trying to tear his hands away from her face.

"Help me hold her," Ellio shouted. "She still needs to breathe it."

Somehow, the two men were able to hold her thrashing limbs long enough for the medicine to disperse. As Ellio was trying to remove the atomizer, her hand clamped around his wrist.

"What... did you...?" she ground out, eyes open to little slits.

"Medicine. We gave you medicine to help," he assured her. "You'll feel better soon."

Her eyes rolled and her hand fell to the cot with a thump. She slumped over, a dead weight in Ellio's arms. He gently laid her back down, pulling the blanket over her.

He let out a breath he didn't realize he'd been holding. She must have passed out again. But the color of her face was already improving. And her breathing was becoming steadier.

He turned to Roscoe, relief flooding his nerves. "Now what?"

"Let her rest. Those things work fast."

"Do you think it'll be enough?"

"You kiddin'? Those things could give a blind man sight, make a deaf man hear. I heard this one fella lost a limb..." At Ellio's audible scoff, Roscoe assented, "Well now, that might be a wee little exaggeratin' on my part. But those Eirenian meds pack a punch. I've heard of people with both feet in the grave crawlin' back out again after throwin' back one of these suckers. Your little lady friend'll be feelin' better in no time. Just needs a good night's rest now."

"She's hardly my friend. I don't even know her name."

"Look there, on the sleeve." Roscoe pointed to her left arm. "Something stitched real fancy-like."

Gingerly, Ellio lifted her arm to examine the writing more closely. In swirling golden letters, it declared, "Property of Retiarius."

The blue-haired young man dropped her arm in shock.

"She's a guild member!"

No Good Deed Goes Unpunished

ELLIO GRUMBLED AND ROLLED over, adjusting his towel for about the hundredth time. He'd tried to make the best of things, pulling a work mat out from under the sling loader, and wadding a couple of towels to serve as a pillow and blanket. But the chill from the floor seeped right through. Half his towels reeked of ergon exhaust fumes, but it was better than nothing. Needless to say, this night was not going as planned.

His mysterious guest woke at one point, startling him from his sleep. Her forehead was beaded with sweat. She squinted down at him in his little nest on the floor, still managing to glare even with her eyes half-closed.

"Water," she commanded. Her voice was raspy and small, but still sharp enough to send Ellio bounding to the sink as if his life depended on it. He tried to help her sit up to drink, but she elbowed him away, sucking greedily from the cup until it was empty, then flopped back onto the cot with a groan.

"A *thank you* would be nice," Ellio muttered, but he could see her chest was already rising and falling slowly in the rhythm of sleep. He eyed the mat and pile of towels that was serving as his bed tonight. Sighing, he ran a hand through his hair. Why couldn't he ever catch a break? His last thought before drifting into a restless sleep was of imperious violet eyes fringed with black bangs.

Darkness still gripped the sky with inky tendrils when Ellio snapped awake the next morning. There was an uncomfortable pressure on his chest. He opened his eyes with a groan and found himself pinned down.

It was a foot.

Correction, not just a foot, *the* foot.

The very foot he had seen peeking out from underneath a dumpster last night. The strange events of yesterday came back to him in a rush and he stared with wide eyes at his mysterious guest. The absurdity of everything made him want to chuckle. He smothered the urge, but some of his wry amusement must have shown on his face because suddenly the foot pressed dangerously on his sternum, cutting off his air.

"Where are we?" the young woman demanded in a quiet voice.

Ellio tried to speak, but only ended up gasping. Rolling her eyes at him, she removed her foot and crossed her arms. He glared at her, but the effect was somewhat lost by his tousled blue hair falling in front of his eyes. Sticking out his lower lip, he raked his hair back with his fingers so that she could appreciate his unpleasant expression.

"Looks like you're feeling better," he mumbled, rubbing the painful spot on his chest.

She didn't say anything, but there was a subtle shift in her stance, like a tiger preparing to pounce. Her sharp stare reminded him that she could knock him flat in an instant. Ellio wisely decided to tone down his attitude.

"I found you under a dumpster behind my shop." She scowled and he held up his hands, palms out. "I swear! I was just taking out the trash and there you were. It was pouring, and you'd crawled underneath." At her raised eyebrow, he cleared his throat.

She was still staring at him, and now she started drumming her fingers along her forearm.

"I tried talking to you, but it was useless. You were way too sick." Ellio took in her narrowed eyes and began speaking faster in his nervousness.

"I couldn't just leave you out there in the rain, so I brought you back to my shop. You were so bad off, my neighbor Roscoe opened an Eirenian atomizer he'd been saving." He took a deep breath.

"You expect me to believe someone like you had an Eirenian atomizer?"

"What's that supposed to mean?" Ellio crossed his arms over his chest.

She shifted her weight, putting one hand on her hip and using the other to make a dismissive gesture of their surroundings.

"Unbelievable," Ellio huffed and stood, brushing the dust off his coveralls. He was at least a foot taller than her when they were both standing. For some reason, this made him feel a little smug. "You're better, aren't you?" he snapped.

In an instant, she was in his face. She yanked on the collar of his shirt, forcing him to bend down until they were eye to eye. Her knuckles twisted into his chest, and Ellio winced. "If you're lying to me, I will break every bone in your body."

"I'm not." Ellio wrenched free from her grip. He could feel a flush creeping up his neck and clapped a hand against it, embarrassed. Taking a step back, he held his hands out in front of him. "I was just trying to help. You can leave at any time. Really, any time now." He gestured helpfully toward the door.

The woman stared at him like he was a moron. "You never answered my question. Where are we?"

"We're in the Downs," Ellio muttered, looking away. "We don't really do street names here."

She hummed in acknowledgment and her eyes scanned the shop.

Ellio cringed as he imagined how it must appear to her. In the rear, a voltsleigh lay with its chassis cracked open, wires piled to the side in a heap. The sling loader in the center was suspended by a pair of rusty crow jacks that had seen better days. Even his toolbox looked pathetic as it squatted in the corner, the dented container leaning slightly to the left.

I look like such a loser.

Ellio rubbed his face, grimacing.

But when he risked a glance at her, he found the young woman was staring curiously at the hybrid rotomotor he'd designed. He'd come up with the idea after watching Ma Logan's hoverchair stall out on Bleecher Hill. This new rotomotor had synchronized ports, allowing the system to continually adjust. No more stalling on steep inclines. It was a nifty little device. Ellio was quite proud of it.

Must be a coincidence, he thought. There's no way she'd know he invented it.

Ellio gave himself a mental shake. "How are you feeling?" he ventured.

"Better." She turned back toward him, a question on her lips.

He smiled and held a hand to his chest. "Ellio." When her noncommittal grunt indicated that she wasn't about to add anything else, he asked, "And you are?"

Her violet eyes flicked to his, and she considered him for a moment. "Kaya," she replied, with reluctance, as if giving a treasure to someone she wasn't sure deserved it.

"Kaya, don't you remember anything about last night? About getting sick?"

She shook her head. "I was at a party, but I went out to get some air. Then it all gets kind of hazy." She rubbed at her temples as if trying to jumpstart her memory. Her stomach rumbled, and she looked away, a faint blush coloring her cheeks.

"You must be hungry. Let me see if I can find you something." Ellio sprang up and started rummaging around in the back of his shop. After a moment, he returned with a pot and lit the Zenon burner. A syrupy smell soon filled the air.

"What is it?" Kaya shouldered him over to peer inside.

"Seriously?" Ellio raised an eyebrow. "Melty O's. The artificial sugar and carbohydrate monstrosity no childhood should be without."

"Hmm." Kaya peered into the pot as he stirred. "It smells sweet." She smiled at him, a genuine smile that stole Ellio's breath away. After a moment, she caught herself and the grin dissolved into a more neutral expression. However, the tension around her eyes seemed somewhat softer than before.

Ellio blinked. "Yeah, they're definitely sweet. Is that okay?"

"Yes," Kaya nodded vigorously, eyes fixed on the pot.

"That's a relief." Ellio chuckled as he looked down again to stir the sticky concoction so that it wouldn't burn. "This is one of the few things I can cook." Curls of steam rose from the pot as he spooned the Melty O's into two mismatched bowls and handed her one.

She sat on the cot, holding the bowl between her hands, and blew on it a few times. Then she crammed a spoonful into her mouth. "This is really good," she mumbled, mouth already full with another bite.

Ellio leaned against his workbench, holding his bowl. "They're delicious, even if they're not super healthy."

For a moment, they ate in comfortable silence.

After scraping the last sticky chunks from her bowl, Kaya set it on his workbench. "I'm leaving." She stretched her hands over her head.

"Back to Retiarius?"

Kaya stiffened. Releasing her hands from her stretch, she turned her back on him completely. "Yes. What of it?"

"Nothing, nothing." Ellio deflated a little, hearing the hostility in her voice. "I'm a fan. Roscoe and I watch the matches sometimes, when we can get his janky old gridscreen to work. I just thought fighters weren't allowed out of the compound without an escort."

She muttered something under her breath. Her fists clenched for a moment, and she huffed, "I'm just staff."

"Okay, I get it." Ellio scratched his neck, feeling awkward. "They must have different rules for you, then. Must be a cool place to work..."

Her deadpan look made him trail off in dismay. Ellio couldn't understand it. Who wouldn't be excited to work for Retiarius? But it was clear she didn't want to talk about it.

Kaya had turned away again, and it felt like a wall of invisible ice had formed between them.

"Thanks for the food." She waved without looking back. "Later."

Ellio scratched his head, staring out the doorway long after she'd disappeared. The greyness of the Downs slipped back over him, like a shroud. How strange. Was it always so gloomy around here? With Kaya, the world had seemed a little brighter, the colors more vivid. Ellio shook his head. He was starting to sound as crazy as old man Roscoe. Must be sleep deprivation.

Still, in a way, it had been fun. But he'd never see her again, right?

Like everything in Retiarius, the dining hall was unnecessarily extravagant. Ornate vaulted ceilings were held up by fluted columns lining either side of the room. Tapestries of historic battles lined the walls, victors holding their bloody spoils.

Kaya barely noticed her surroundings as she grabbed her breakfast tray and slid onto a bench at one of the empty tables. She stared dismally at her food and poked at the slab of unsalted moj fish. The fermented brown bean soup smelled awful. Kaya grunted and began spooning the soup into her mouth through a sheer act of will. The quicker she ate it, the quicker she could leave.

She hated the spectacle and social gathering of mealtimes in Retiarius. Amid a sea of pink chiffons and stretchy neon fabrics, she alone was dressed in a plain black jumpsuit.

Just who are they trying to impress? There aren't any cameras here.

But the girls seemed just as anxious to vie for attention among their peers as their patrons. Kaya wrinkled her nose. *Disgusting.* She speared the moj fish and forced herself to swallow the slimy mass on her tongue.

A novice walked toward Kaya's table. Kaya pinned the girl with a ferocious glare. "Don't even think about it," she growled.

The girl gulped and scampered away.

"That's Kaya," another girl whispered to the novice. "She always eats alone."

Kaya smirked into her soup. *At least these nitwits can get one thing right.* She could hear the girls shuffling around at the table behind her. It was overcrowded and girls were squirming to keep from falling off the bench.

Kaya didn't care. She ate alone.

Twittering laughter rolled in from the entrance and Kaya rolled her eyes.

It was Stiletto and her crowd of parasites. The buxom brunette had quite a following at Retiarius. Kaya was baffled by it. She eyed Stiletto with disdain. The young woman was a foolish and incompetent fighter. She let her emotions get in the way. Kaya had heard she'd lost her mask in the ring after just three matches. But somehow, she was able to maintain a place in the guild despite that.

Maybe there's more to her than meets the eye.

Kaya studied her for a moment. Stiletto approached a table, one of her cling-ons carrying a tray of food for her. The table was filled with novices and untested fighters, who looked at Stiletto and her entourage with admiration. They scooted down, making room for her to sit.

Stiletto looked down her nose at them, flicking her wrist in disdain. "Move," she demanded.

The girls scattered like cherry blossoms in the breeze. Stiletto's crew laughed as they fled.

Kaya snorted into her bean soup.

Big fish in a little pond.

Was Stiletto glaring at her? For a moment, Kaya saw the brunette's eyes dart to her, filled with anger. Interesting. Kaya tried to catch her at it again, but Stiletto was absorbed in giggling with her teammates or purring coquettishly in someone's ear.

Kaya clenched her spoon. Maybe she was too dismissive of the other girls. After last night, she needed to take stock of her surroundings. Everything after the party was a blur. Kaya refused to admit how much that scared her. She hated being helpless. The feeling reminded her of the day she'd been left in a tent as a child and told to wait until it was safe.

She'd promised herself never to be that weak again. But just this morning, she'd woken up, tucked snugly in a strange man's cot. Totally helpless.

Kaya ground her teeth together.

I messed up, missed something. Why can't I remember what happened last night?

She was lost in her thoughts when someone shoved her roughly in the shoulder.

"Sorry, Kaya, I didn't see you there," Stiletto laughed as she walked by.

Kaya leaped out of her seat and pinned Stiletto's right arm behind her back. "What makes you think you can touch me?" Kaya growled.

"Can't you take a joke, you freak?" Stiletto hissed back.

Kaya jerked her arm viciously.

"Ow, stop it! You're hurting me!" Stiletto shrieked.

"That's the point, *idiot*." Venom dripped from Kaya's words.

"Kaya, enough!" A voice boomed from the entrance. It was Tarak, the guild boss. He must have been doing his morning inspections.

Could Stiletto have timed this?

Kaya narrowed her eyes, but released Stiletto, shoving her away.

It would have been satisfying to see the brunette fall on her face, but Stiletto was graceful. She caught herself mid stumble and turned back to glare at Kaya. "Wake up on the wrong side of the bed today, little savage?" She jeered, flipping her long curls over her shoulder. The girls with her snickered.

"What's with her?" another novice whispered.

Kaya slammed her hands on the table. Curse Tarak and his timing! She shoved her tray away, fuming. It slid across the table and clattered to the floor. Some of the girls at the next table flinched and turned to gape at her.

Storming back to her room, people jumped out of Kaya's path.

Kaya was shaking with anger. Her fingers fumbled at the latch of her door. Furious, she wrenched it open, then slammed it closed.

How dare Stiletto? Who does she think she is? She'd never last two minutes with me in the arena.

I hate them. Those stupid girls, prancing around like a brainless herd of sagrin. Pathetic.

But as Kaya's thoughts drifted to Stiletto, she frowned. Yesterday, someone had got the better of her and today Stiletto was picking a fight out of the blue. Could the two be connected?

Kaya flung herself onto her bed and pounded her pillow, imagining Stiletto's smirking face and twittering laugh.

Could anyone be that vapid? Maybe it's just an act. The timing aligned perfectly with Tarak's morning inspection. Was it a contingency plan?

Kaya growled, black fingernails gouging into the pillow.

Whether it was Stiletto or not, something had left Kaya with memory gaps she couldn't explain. She'd been at the spring soiree last night.

Normally, she hated any kind of formal functions, but Retiarius parties were one of the few opportunities fighters had of skirting around the guild's strict dietary rules.

There's only so much moj fish anyone should be forced to eat. Kaya grimaced at the thought of the slimy white fish, renowned for its protein and lack of fats.

Was it something she had eaten at the party? Something slipped in her drink? But Kaya was always careful.

She groaned into her pillow. Kaya knew about the competition at Retiarius. As an undefeated fighter, she had special privileges, but her name wasn't revealed to the public.

Only the guild members know my identity, Kaya thought, *but someone targeted me last night.*

Still, she couldn't avoid guild parties forever, and she certainly couldn't stop eating and drinking. Kaya was already distant enough with the other girls as it was. She couldn't go much further without calling undue attention to herself. The only way she'd managed to stay sane was through her nightly excursions sneaking out into the city of Beulah. She couldn't jeopardize what little freedom she'd carved out for herself by arousing suspicion now.

Thoughts of food drew her mind back to the sugary sweet taste of Melty O's and Ellio's smile as he held the bowl out to her. Kaya shook her head, but her mind kept replaying images of his face.

She recalled the tightness around his eyes, the concern woven in his voice. "Don't you remember anything about last night?" he'd asked her. Kaya had been completely helpless, and he'd taken care of her. There weren't many people who would do that, especially without expecting something in return.

Kaya knew she'd been fortunate. The night could have gone very differently if someone less amiable had found her. Thinking about it made her skin crawl.

And the Downs of all places. How on Elorah did I wind up there?

Her mind was racing, but she quickly grew frustrated by her inability to find answers that made sense.

"That's it!" She shoved herself off the bed and grabbed her ruewood staff. "I need to hit something." She whipped the door open with a crash and stormed off to the training area.

The day passed in a haze of sweaty, tiring work. The Downs were humid after it rained, and Ellio couldn't afford a climate regulator in his shop. He had to rely solely on the open garage bay door and a small fan. Ellio stoutly avoided looking at his cot, where he could still picture a dark-haired young woman, snuggling against his pillow.

Finished for the day, he headed to the back room and doused himself off with a cold shower. Feeling refreshed, he threw on a clean shirt, toweled off his hair, and headed over to Roscoe's.

"Still alive, old man?" Ellio called out as he pushed aside the curtains of the noodle bar.

"Lousy brat," Roscoe snapped back, but he was grinning as he waved Ellio in.

Ellio slid onto one of the rickety bar stools and leaned his elbow on the chipped counter. Roscoe pushed a bowl of pork noodles to him.

Ellio sniffed appreciatively. "Thanks."

"Don't mention it, kid."

Ellio grinned and turned on the gridscreen, rigged up in the corner. Images flickered off and on for a moment before it settled into focus. Ellio tuned in to the live streaming Retiarius match. Right now, it was a pair battle. Fan favorites Stiletto and Charmyn were teamed up against the Twins, Drynn and Lorelai.

Retiarius was an all-female fighters guild, but they would fight male and female champions from other cities and regions of Elorah.

Ellio slurped his noodles and watched the twins leap around gracefully, trying to catch Charmyn in their net.

Roscoe coughed and sidled up to him. "So, how'd it go?" he whispered.

Ellio gave him a sidelong glance. "What?"

The old man grunted and puffed out his whiskered cheeks. "So that's how it is? Rip an old man from his few hours of blessed sleep and leave him hanging out to dry."

Ellio looked away, stirring his noodles. "What're you talking about?" he muttered.

"The girl! What happened to her?" Roscoe exploded in impatience.

Ellio hunched further over his bowl. Violet eyes danced before his vision, framed by black bangs. A spine-chilling glare. A shy smile half hidden by a steaming bowl of Melty O's. He frowned. "Nothing happened. She woke up, and she left."

Roscoe threw down his towel. "And?"

"And nothing, that's it. She's from Aurea. It's not like she wanted to be in the Downs." Ellio felt himself bristling a little. What did Roscoe expect?

"So, you blew it?"

"I did not!" Ellio clenched his chopsticks, knuckles turning white.

"Beautiful girls don't fall out of the sky every day, you know?"

Roscoe was eyeing him with something like pity and it made Ellio bite out, "She didn't fall out of the sky, she crawled under a dumpster."

"You should've talked to her. You're a nice kid, Ellio. Might've made a friend."

Ellio's eyes flashed. "Yeah, right. I can see it now, being some rich chick's pet project. Thanks, I'll pass." He slurped the last of his broth and set the bowl down roughly on the counter.

"Suit yourself," Roscoe huffed and turned away to wipe down the stove. Ellio distinctly heard him mutter, "Young fool."

He took a deep breath and held out a hand in peace. "Look, can we just drop it? Silent Nyte's about to come on."

"That little wisp of a thing?" Roscoe called over his shoulder. "Don't know what you see in her."

Ellio thought about the graceful fighter. Dressed in black, wearing a twisted demon mask with long curved horns. Retiarius allowed its fighters to design their own masks. As long as they remained undefeated, fighters wore a mask in the ring, their identity a secret from the public. "There's something about her, Roscoe. She holds herself like a champion."

"Bah!" Roscoe scoffed, but Ellio noticed with satisfaction that he was heading back over to watch the match.

"I'm serious, old man. Watch how she moves, like she owns the sand. All the other fighters are chump change compared to her."

They both leaned closer as Silent Nyte entered the arena, her mask already in place.

The announcer was setting up the match, whipping the audience into a frenzy. His bronze face was superimposed over the arena sand as a gigantic hologram. "We have a very special match for you tonight. Our own angel of darkness, Silent Nyte, versus the undefeated champion of the north, Oblido." The announcer stretched out the last syllable of Oblido's name and it echoed around the arena, making Roscoe's gridscreen crackle.

Ellio gulped. The man was three times her size at least, and more beast than human. Oblido ripped open his shirt, exposing muscular shoulders covered in shaggy hair. Jagged teeth protruded from his bulging lower lip.

"Isn't that the guy who destroyed Nagata's spine last season?" Roscoe leaned over the counter.

How could they send another woman against this guy?

Oblido was a brute. He relished disabling fighters for life and boasted about how many careers he'd ended with his signature move "Whiplash." Supposedly, his name meant "Crush" in one of the forgotten languages.

Ellio dug his nails into his thighs, eyes fixed on Silent Nyte. How would she react?

Faced with the slender female Retiarius fighter, Oblido hooted with laughter. He even turned his back to her, making rude comments to the audience.

Ellio winced. Turning your back on an opponent in the arena was the worst kind of stupid. But Silent Nyte didn't take advantage of the golden opportunity. Instead, she waited, tapping her boot in the sand until Oblido turned back toward her. She threw her weapon aside, an extendable staff with polished silver caps, and launched into a front handspring. Flipped herself upward. Caught her thighs around Oblido's neck, and threw him to the sand. The earth-shattering force made the cameras rattle.

Her thighs cinched around Oblido's throat. His face rapidly turned purple. He clawed at her. Silent Nyte gave an open-handed chop behind his left ear. Oblido fell, knocked unconscious. A roar of applause rose from the audience.

Silent Nyte dusted herself off and flipped up her staff with a toe. She twirled it around and snapped it back into place at her side before heading for the exit.

Ellio stiffened as he watched her walk off. The way that she moved seemed familiar. He was surprised to find himself thinking about Kaya again. But there was no way. She said she was just a staff member. Unbidden, her violet eyes and serious expression flitted through his mind. Ellio propped his cheek in his hand and leaned on the counter. *I wonder what Kaya's doing tonight.*

Silent Nyte had ended her match in record time. The announcer scrambled to fill the minutes before the next match. They showed a breakdown of the fight, slo-mo reels of her front handspring. Ellio couldn't get over how incredible she was. He gushed at Roscoe until the old man couldn't take it anymore and sent him packing.

Ellio whistled on the way back to his shop. There wasn't much to look forward to in the Downs but seeing Silent Nyte inspired him. Maybe someday he'd be able to face the giants in his life.

He heard someone snicker and looked around, startled.

It was Naruna, a local thug making the rounds through his corner of the Downs, shaking up local businesses for his "protection." Stores paid to keep him and his thugs from raiding their merchandise and scaring off customers. It was effective, at least most of the time.

"There you are, twerp," Naruna jeered.

Next to Ellio's tall, slender frame, Naruna appeared short and stout. He kept his orange hair cropped short, with triangular patterns shaved into his scalp. A tight neon-green T-shirt stretched over his muscular chest. The sleeves were ripped off, the better to display his massive biceps. Naruna leaned over the chrome bumper of a voltsleigh and flexed his arm with a grin. When he smiled, the gold certa-dents replacing his two front teeth flashed in the sun.

He gestured to the three lackeys following him. "Check these guns. Bicep curls really payin' off."

Ellio refrained from rolling his eyes. The gangster had a short fuse and a streak of insecurity a stadia long. Any perceived disrespect would trigger a physical confrontation. Violence was all that Naruna seemed to understand. Ellio had given up trying to hold a conversation with him long ago. Naruna and his crew weren't the most intelligent bunch, but what they lacked in ingenuity, they compensated for with brute strength.

"Your account's due, grease monkey," Naruna announced, picking his ear.

Ellio let out a short breath and headed to his cupboard, grabbing enough cash to satiate his neighbor. He set aside a special amount each week, exclusively for these "visits." Naruna was a menace, but at least he was predictable.

After grabbing the cash from Ellio, Naruna punched him in the arm, hard enough to leave a mark. "That's a good little twerp. See ya next time."

With a nod to his mindless entourage, Naruna sauntered out of the shop. One of his cronies slapped a tray on the workbench, sending lug nuts and washers flying.

"Gimme a break," Ellio grumbled. "It took forever to organize those."

His complaint was met with mocking laughter as the thugs ambled out into the night.

Ellio stooped and began cleaning. What was wrong with Naruna? Life in the Downs was rough, but how about some solidarity, for Dral's sake?

It was hard to believe they'd grown up together, scrambling down fire escapes, playing hide and seek in the moldy cardboard boxes littering the alleys. They used to admire the jetbikes parked outside Krodie's Bar, memorizing the specs of their favorite models, dreaming up new color combinations for the ergon engines. Naruna had wanted to be a racer once.

Now look at the two of them. Ellio shook his head, dumping the last of the washers back onto the tray. Naruna was a small-time crook, and Ellio struggled to keep his dad's business afloat. It wouldn't take much to send him off to the debtor's quarry. Making payments to Naruna certainly didn't help.

Maybe he should confront Naruna? Refuse to pay anything else.

But then Ellio remembered Shona, the fiery little woman who used to have a bakery around the corner. Shona's sweet rolls and sesame loaves drew crowds from all over the Downs. She'd refused to pay Naruna, said he was just a punk kid. Then, one day, the windows of her business were nailed shut. A neighbor claimed she saw Shona leaving, beat up real bad.

No one knew where the baker had gone. The smell of fresh bread lingered for a few days around her shop; like a cloud of reproach for those who did nothing to help. But the scent soon faded, choked out by exhaust fumes, sewage, and the overwhelming stench of despair.

Ellio let out a long breath. Confronting Naruna was a nice dream, but who was he kidding? Gutter rats didn't get happy endings.

THE WAY TO A MAN'S HEART

"THAT SHOULD DO IT." Ellio closed the side panel of the hoverchair and gave it a pat. The new rotomotor he'd installed purred happily inside. "It shouldn't give you any more trouble going uphill."

"Such a sweet young man," Ma Logan crooned at him. "I can't tell you how much I appreciate your help." The old woman pushed herself up from her stool with the help of a knobby wooden cane. She tottered toward Ellio, smiling. "I hope you like zucchini muffins."

"I like everything you bake, Ma Logan."

She tittered and began rummaging through her carpet bag. "Young flatterer," she scolded, her eyes sparkling with mischief. "This is an old family recipe. My grandmother passed it down." Ma Logan held a conspiratorial hand to her lips. "Spiced vanilla is the secret." She held out a wax paper bag. The delicious aroma of fresh muffins filled the air.

"Thank you!" Ellio took the bag and helped Ma Logan into her hoverchair.

The old woman settled her bag on her lap and clicked the hoverchair into first gear. Maglev coils hummed to life, and the chair began to float.

"Thank you, dearie." She guided the chair toward the open garage door.

Ellio trailed her to the entryway. "Come by again if it gives you any trouble."

Ma Logan waved as her hoverchair chugged slowly down the street.

"Zucchini muffins?" a skeptical feminine voice spoke up beside him.

Ellio nearly jumped out of his skin. He whirled around, mouth open. Kaya was lounging against the wall, making little circles in the dust with her shoe.

"Kaya! You scared me!" Ellio clutched his chest and released a deep breath. He took in her posture and the patterns traced in the dirt around her boots—boots that must be worth fifty drakka at least. "How long have you been waiting?"

"Not long." She slung a sleek black podpack off her shoulder and dropped it on the ground. Unzipping it, she pulled out a paper bag and thrust it at him. "I wanted to give you this."

"For me?" He took the bag awkwardly and peeked inside. After a quick glance at its contents, Ellio burst out laughing. "This is great, Kaya. Thank you. I was running low on Melty O's."

The bag held at least five boxes. If he could resist the temptation to gorge on their sugary goodness, this could last him a long time.

Kaya huffed and scuffed the ground with the toe of her boot. Today she was wearing heavy black eyeliner. It rimmed her violet eyes and curved out into a shape like webbed bat wings on either side, surrounded by a haze of glimmering red-and-gold eye shadow.

She was beautiful.

After their rocky start, Kaya began dropping by his shop. Ellio had quit trying to predict the timing of these visits. Kaya would materialize soundlessly at his side. Or, he'd look up from his work to find her draped along his cot, bopping her foot to her audiojack. She followed no rational schedule, at least none he could work out. But they'd settled into a comfortable routine of sorts. She was surprisingly easy to be around, and Ellio found himself growing bolder in her presence.

"I was just about to go eat," Ellio blurted and then mentally facepalmed. Real smooth Maestro.

"Okay."

She turned to leave, but Ellio reached out and grabbed her elbow. "Wait, what I meant was, would you like to come with me? To eat?"

Kaya looked at him, burrow furrowed. "In the *Downs*?"

"Why not? We may not have table cloths, five-crown restaurants, or basic hygiene, but what we lack in those areas we make up with..." He scanned the area, trying to think. "Good company." He flashed a sheepish grin.

Kaya eyed him for a moment, in which Ellio felt sure he had just failed magnificently. But then, his eyes widened at her murmur of acquiescence.

"Great!" Ellio wanted to slap himself. Could he be more obvious? Kaya visited him frequently but today she looked skittish. Like she was ready to bolt at a moment's notice. He should pick somewhere close. Who was he kidding? The only place he could afford was Roscoe's and besides, the old man would get a kick out of meeting her again. His rainy day.

As soon as Ellio pushed aside the bedraggled curtains of the noodle bar, Roscoe began his heckling. But he cut off abruptly as he caught sight of Kaya slipping in behind Ellio.

Roscoe spluttered for a minute, but soon found his tongue. "If it isn't Sleepin' Beauty. Sorry you found this chump instead of a prince."

"Hey, come on! I'm charming." Ellio protested.

"Ha!" Roscoe shook a wooden spoon at him. "Don't bet on it, kid."

Ellio slid onto one of the bar stools at the counter. When he noticed Kaya hanging around uncertainly in the doorway, he patted the stool next to him. "It's okay, Kaya. Honestly, he's not that bad. Can't say the same about his cooking, though."

"Kids today got no respect," Roscoe muttered, ladling broth into two bowls. Using two long cooking sticks like pincers, he lowered a bundle of noodles into each bowl. "Can't even complain to your parents anymore."

Kaya drifted over cautiously and perched on the stool next to Ellio. She folded her hands in her lap and crossed her ankles together. But at Roscoe's words, she tilted her head, giving Ellio a sidelong glance.

"Your parents?" she asked softly.

Ellio reached up and squeezed the goggles he always wore around his throat. The worn leather straps were soft against his palm. "They passed away. Mom when I was a baby and Dad eight winters back."

Roscoe placed two bowls in front of them.

Ellio turned his bowl in a circle, blowing on the soup. "Just life, I guess." He toyed with the paper wrapper of his chopsticks, folding it into little squares and then stretching it out like an accordion. When he realized she was watching, Ellio crumpled the wrapper into a ball and set it on the counter. Turning to Kaya, he asked, "What about your parents? Not many people get the opportunity to work for Retiarius."

"They're gone." Kaya's voice was hard. "I'm in the guild's debt." She snapped her chopsticks open and stirred her soup.

"I'm sorry."

"They were weak, so they died." Kaya shrugged and speared a boiled egg in her bowl.

Ellio was silent for a moment. How was he supposed to respond to that? He propped his cheek in his palm. Then he realized something.

"Ah-ha!" He jabbed his finger at Kaya.

She bristled like a cat and the half-eaten egg plopped back into the broth. Glaring at him, she opened her mouth, probably to scold him, but Roscoe beat her to it.

"You fool, boy! What're you yellin' about? Nearly gave me a stroke!"

"You, you!" Ellio swung the accusing finger at Roscoe. "You have hard-boiled eggs? Never in all the times I've eaten here have you ever given me an egg."

"What d'you expect when you pay in *chores*?" Roscoe put his hands on his hips and jutted out his bristly chin.

"I fixed your stove, old man! And your climate regulator! And just about everything that runs on energy cells in this shop!"

"Them eggs are for *payin'* customers," Roscoe said with a glare. "Payin' customers that bathe every once in a while."

Ellio spluttered in indignation. Banging his hands on the counter, he used them to lean over the edge into Roscoe's face. "Look here, *old* man, you wouldn't even have customers—"

Ellio's retort was interrupted by a small chirrup. Both he and Roscoe looked at Kaya, whose face was fixed on the floor, eyes shrouded by her long bangs. Her shoulders were shaking, a hand clasped over her mouth.

"Kaya, are you all right?" Ellio reached toward her and she looked up, laughter spilling from her lips, eyes sparkling.

Both men blinked, surprised by her sudden outburst.

Still chuckling, Kaya wiped her eye with the side of her finger. "Definitely good company," she said, smiling.

Ellio promptly forgot what he had been so annoyed about.

Kaya's smile could light up the sun. It was radiant and beautiful, but there was also something fragile to it. Like a young bird tumbling out of its nest for the first time. It was almost as if she was learning how to smile, and Ellio had an instinctive desire to protect her joy at all costs.

As they slurped their noodles, Roscoe wiped down the inside of the counter with a dubious-looking rag. "You young kids are impressed by Retiarius, but in my day, all we wanted to hear were stories about the warriors of Eiren."

"Ah, come on, Roscoe. Not that old nonsense," Ellio groaned.

Beside him, Kaya perked up. "I'd like to hear," she objected.

"Don't encourage him, Kaya." Ellio waved his hands in warning, but Roscoe gave a triumphant grin.

"Now, now, the lady has spoken." Roscoe set down his rag and pulled a stool over on his side of the bar. "The warriors of Eiren were special.

Some folk say they could live hundreds of years, filled with a supernatural power."

Ellio sighed dramatically. When Kaya's eyes flashed to his, he winked at her. "Here we go again."

Roscoe raised his chin, huffing, and continued. "An Eirenian warrior could take on hundreds of opponents; their arms were like molten steel, cuttin' through enemies. Their mystical power burned like a blue flame. Powerful beyond imagining."

"And how many years has it been since anyone's seen one of these flaming warriors?" Ellio drawled.

"Eiren's withdrawn to its own borders. They have an ancient prophecy that great warriors will arise in a time of darkness. When there's a great need, they'll appear. Warriors fueled by the power that slumbers within every heart; the power of the spirit."

"Come on, enough fairy tales," Ellio grumbled.

Kaya reached over and knuckle-punched his forearm. Her gaze was rapt on Roscoe. "Have you ever seen one?"

"Once, when I was young."

"Now you've done it," Ellio said petulantly, rubbing the sore spot on his arm.

Roscoe ignored him. "Was a fire in Beulah, long ago. Downs was all mud n' thatch then. Some fool knocked over an oil lamp. Set the whole neighborhood ablaze. I was just a nipper, but I saw him. A man, awash in blue fire. 'Cept the flames didn't burn him. Hauled my brother n' me outta the blaze. Folks whispered about it. Lotta kids tellin' the same crazy tale. Don't make no sense. Houses hotter n' a furnace, and he walked in like it were nothin'. I still remember those blue flames, all twisted up around, like it was listenin' to him. Never seen nothin' like it."

"Probably hallucinations from inhaling too much smoke," Ellio muttered.

Kaya elbowed him. "My parents used to tell me stories about Eiren when we lived on the plains of Alsehir. Before—" Her voice cut off abruptly and she put a hand to her mouth.

"Before what, Kaya?" Ellio asked.

"Never mind." She shook her head and returned her attention to the soup. "I don't know why I brought it up."

Roscoe frowned and made a show of turning around to wipe down the stove.

Ellio ran a hand through his hair. It felt like something was squirming in his stomach, but for once he couldn't blame Roscoe's noodles. It was like a tiny invisible thread was being wound around his heart, squeezing it. And he had the inexplicable sensation that if he could pull on that thread and follow it, it would lead him to wherever Kaya was.

She stood and placed her chopsticks carefully across the rim of the bowl. "Thanks for the food. I need to get going." She turned and slipped through the shop curtains.

Ellio's eyes followed her out, bewildered, while Roscoe looked down at her bowl.

"Dang, Ellio. Look! Your princess slipped three gold drakka on the table. It's too much. Go after her and give this back."

"Kaya, wait!" Ellio shouted and jumped out of his chair, completely forgetting to take the drakka Roscoe was holding out to him. "Wait, Kaya. Please." He sprinted out after her.

Dusk had taken hold of the Downs. The streets were lit by the buzzing glow of cheap neon signs. Shadows of people twisted around the corners; bellowing laughter echoed through the alleyway. Ellio strained his eyes, searching for a glimpse of Kaya's petite silhouette. He banged his fist against the wall. She'd vanished again.

The entrance to Retiarius was an elaborate gate that arched and curled in whimsical wrought-iron flourishes, gilded in gold. But Kaya didn't use the main entrance. Fighters were supposed to remain in the compound unless escorted. Leaving the compound on her own meant sneaking in and out.

On the surface at least, Retiarius claimed that these rules existed for the benefit of the fighters. A disgruntled punter would sometimes try to injure a guild member who cost them money. Or offer money for fighters to throw a match. Retiarius was a guild with a long-standing reputation as a trustworthy betting hall. Members who had attempted to fix a match often wound up missing a limb, or worse.

Kaya ran along the roof ridges, as quiet as a shadow. Dragul hadn't just taught her survival skills. Combat, stealth, and infiltration were also a part of her repertoire that she found increasingly useful.

In some of her darker musings, Kaya wondered if Dragul had been raising her to be an assassin. He'd never clarified what exactly her training was for. Always going on about honor and discipline. Until their quarrel, when he left her high and dry in Beulah.

That old fossil.

Kaya clenched her fists. If she ever saw him again, she was going to throttle him. He wouldn't be able to get the best of her next time. She'd learned a few new tricks from her time in the arena.

Dragul's disapproving frown played in her memory. Who cared what he thought? Violence was the only way to get through to some people. And being an assassin had a certain appeal.

But seeing the way Ellio smiled at her, Kaya was glad she'd never had to ruthlessly end someone's life. Maybe she could try something other than fighting once her Retiarius contract was paid. She shook her head against such sentimentality. Musing was not like her.

Slipping onto the ledge of the lower guild roof, Kaya shimmied up the drainpipe until she reached her room. Being an undefeated fighter came with privileges. She had her own room. It was small, but private. And the window access presented all the freedom she required, with or without the guild's approval.

Normally, she stayed along the rooftops, watching the people of Beulah from above. A silent spectator to the unending conflicts and drama of the city roiling beneath her. Other guild members used their free time for shopping trips. With an escort, Retiarius members could access the most exclusive areas of Beulah. But the glamor of Aurea held no pull for Kaya. She preferred to spend her time alone. If she wasn't exploring, she was training.

As Kaya slid stealthily into the room, she heard a slight rustle of fabric. Someone was lurking outside her door. On silent feet, she stalked over and flung it open. A woman stumbled backward from her doorway, curly brown hair tumbling around her shoulders in waves.

Stiletto.

"Oh, Kaya, you're awake? The other girls told me you were resting."

"I'm finished," Kaya said dryly. The brunette was getting to be a nuisance. "Why are you here, Stiletto?"

"Just passing by." Stiletto smiled innocently at her. "I thought I heard the sound of a window closing and wanted to make sure no undesirables were creeping about."

Kaya nodded slowly; threat acknowledged. Stiletto had a suspicion that she was slipping out and now here she was skulking around for proof. Thankfully, Kaya had returned in time, but she couldn't be so careless in the future.

"So glad you're feeling okay," Stiletto purred. She flipped her hair over her shoulder and sashayed down the hall.

Kaya closed the door and banged her forehead against it. That was close. Too close. She needed to be more careful.

Stiletto was a few years older than Kaya. Maybe she was insecure about being usurped. The brunette might be a mediocre fighter, but she made up for it with cunning. Fighting with a partner in paired matches show-cased her best features and hid the worst. Her risqué outfits, voluptuous figure, and ruthlessness in the arena made her a crowd favorite. Cheers always rocked the stadium when she stepped onto the sand.

There was a reason Retiarius members often hung in cliques. Being part of a group made it harder for sabotage and even murder by a jealous guildmate. No one talked about it openly, but Kaya had been suspicious ever since Unya disappeared. When Kaya had entered Retiarius, Unya was a skilled fighter rising through the ranks. Then one day, she was wracked with painful stomach bleeding. The alleged cause? Bad fruit. Retiarius investigations claimed an exotic fruit from the market con-tained a rare strain of stomach worm. It nested in its victim's bowels, causing excruciating pain and ultimately death if left untreated. The guild had deep coffers, but it was also a very practical organization. A relatively new talent was hardly worth the exorbitant medical fees. The girl had quietly disappeared one night.

Kaya had a dark sense that Unya had been purposefully eliminated. But she had no proof. Just a feeling in her gut. Nothing overtly traced back to Stiletto, either. But now that idiot was hanging around outside Kaya's room. Like she was waiting for Kaya to slip up.

Perhaps Stiletto was more deadly outside the arena than in it.

Kaya pressed two fingers to the crease forming between her eyebrows. Great, now she was starting to get a headache. It was risky to keep visiting Ellio. An unnecessary risk. Repeatedly visiting the same place was just begging to get caught.

A vision of Ellio's smiling face rose in her mind. She could picture him clearly, leaning over his workbench, scribbling calculations for his next project. Biting his lip as he mentally calculated an obscure formula for intake compression. She snorted in amusement. He was fun to observe.

When she'd first started visiting him, Ellio would flutter around his shop, rearranging tools, sweeping up metal shavings, or fighting a losing battle with the oil stains that dotted his floor. All the while stealing glances at her while she lounged on his cot. Kaya liked to catch him at it. She'd flip through an old magazine or listen to music on her audiojack, and when she knew he was watching, flick her gaze upward to pin him with a stare of her own. He'd splutter and blush and vigorously return to cleaning. But gradually he'd become more comfortable in her presence. Now he would work on projects sometimes. Kaya liked the way his brow furrowed when he concentrated and the way he'd practically glow with excitement when describing one of his inventions.

Kaya caught herself smiling fondly and sat up with a jolt. How ridiculous! To be daydreaming about a guy from the Downs. Maybe she was coming down with something?

Kaya held a hand to her forehead, but everything felt normal. She'd always had a strong constitution but after that Eirenian atomizer, it almost felt like she could fly. Kaya stretched out her hand, curling her fingers into a tiger claw strike and then a palm strike. She grabbed her staff and headed for the door. Training for a few hours would help clear her head.

TAKING OUT THE TRASH

OIL SPLATTERED ACROSS HIS cheek. Ellio sucked in a breath and squeezed the torque wrench until the metal bit into his hand. He was sorely tempted to chuck it at the wall. Nothing was going right today. Rusty lug nuts refused to budge even after he coated them in grease. Ma Logan's hoverchair was acting up again. He'd adjusted the alignment at least five times now but she still complained that it pulled a little to the left. And now a routine oil change was turning into a disaster.

It had been two weeks since Kaya's last visit. Not that Ellio was counting. She'd stopped in frequently after their meal at Roscoe's but now it was like she'd dropped off the planet. Ellio missed her. He was afraid she was never coming back, afraid that he'd never see her again. Worse, there was no way for him to contact her. People from the Downs weren't welcome in districts like Aurea, especially not in the center where Retiarius was located. With his grease-splattered clothes, they would never allow him to pass through the gates into Beulah's wealthier city districts.

What if I never see her again?

The plastic cap he was turning slipped out of his grip and rolled away. He craned his neck to see where it had gone and clocked his head, *hard*, against the rear axle.

"Dral!" he yelled, and this time he really did fling his torque wrench.

"Is everything okay down there?" Two sandaled feet with lime-green nail polish stepped into view, followed by Kaya's head as she bent to peer under the chassis at Ellio. Her bangs slipped in front of her eyes. "You seem upset."

"Kaya!" Ellio exclaimed and promptly bumped his head a second time. "Oww!" He rolled out from under the vehicle, rubbing his head. "It's great to see you. I..." He felt heat creeping up his neck.

Kaya tilted her head, bangs flopping over her left eye. She was so cute.

Ellio swallowed. He steeled himself and blurted out, "I missed you."

She gave him a shy smile and suddenly the bump on his head didn't seem so bad.

After he had gotten cleaned up, Ellio made them a batch of Melty O's. Kaya had quite the sweet tooth and couldn't get enough of the sticky concoction. Her eyes always lit up hopefully when he pulled out his Zenon burner.

He was scraping the last sugary bit from the side of his bowl with the spoon, when she asked, "How long have you been a mechanic?"

"Pretty much my whole life. I can't remember a time when I wasn't tinkering around with one kind of machine or other. My dad taught me. Hoped we'd keep the business running together. Hence the sign 'Aubri and Son.'" He thumbed at the sign above the entrance to the shop.

"So, you've always known what you wanted to do?" Kaya hugged her arms around her legs, resting her chin on her knees.

"Well, it's my day job."

"Day job?" Her voice was puzzled.

"You know, what I do to get by, well, sort of anyway." He smiled sheepishly. "But rather than fix broken machines, I'd like to build new ones. Like that rotomotor I built for Ma Logan. Or the new jetbike engine I designed."

"Jetbike engine?"

"I have it in the shop. Wanna see?"

Kaya nodded, her expression curious.

Ellio rubbed his hands together, grinning, and sauntered over to a vehicle covered with a faded gray tarp. "I'm gonna call her 'Silent Nyte' after the Retiarius fighter." He whipped off the tarp with a flourish.

Kaya broke into a coughing fit. When Ellio looked back in concern, she waved him off. "I'm fine. Just swallowed funny." Setting her bowl on the workbench, she joined him by the jetbike. "Looks fast."

"She will be." Ellio nodded, patting her fuel tank lovingly. "By the time I'm through, she'll be the fastest thing on three wheels around here."

Kaya's hand hovered over the handlebars, and she looked up at him.

"Go on," Ellio encouraged. "You can check her out. She won't bite. I've got the power disconnected."

Kaya slung her leg over the side and pulled herself onto the bike with feline grace.

I bet she's a good dancer, Ellio thought with a blush.

She toggled through the controls, flipping the startup switches with familiarity.

"Bit of a racer yourself?" He leaned back against the workbench, smiling.

"I dabble." She grinned, testing the throttle. The machine sputtered to life, lurching forward about a foot before the ignition cut out. Kaya's jaw dropped open in surprise, and she tumbled off the jetbike. Ellio tried to catch her and they rolled to the floor in a disordered tangle of limbs.

Kaya peeled herself off him. "You said the power was disconnected! Some mechanic *you* are!" She punctuated her words with a punch to his chest.

It hurt more than Ellio wanted to admit. He rubbed his chest indignantly. "It should have been. I disconnected the ignition coil." He scratched his head. "Or at least I *thought* I did." His fingertips traced along her forearm to her elbow with a featherlight touch. "Are you hurt?"

At her incredulous stare, he started to chuckle. Soon they were both laughing and gasping for breath.

"You are ridiculous," she huffed, but Ellio could tell she was fighting to maintain her glare. Amusement brightened her eyes as she leaned closer to whisper, "But also, a little cute." She held up her thumb and index finger to indicate the smidgeon of cuteness he possessed.

"Thank you?" His voice trailed off in a question. Ellio wasn't quite sure whether she meant it as a compliment. But his thoughts were derailed by a sudden realization. Somehow their faces had gotten very close. Ellio could see flecks of lighter purple in the center of her deep-violet eyes. He found he couldn't look away.

Kaya laughed once more and tweaked his nose. "Or maybe clueless." She shuffled around so that she was sitting cross-legged on the floor, her knees brushing against his.

Ellio grinned and gave her his best puppy dog look. "Come on, cut me some slack."

"What kind of mechanic doesn't know how to properly disconnect an ignition coil?"

"An overworked, exhausted mechanic who rescues strangers in the night."

"A melodramatic tradesman. Please spare me." She held a hand to her forehead.

"What have we here?" a disparaging voice interrupted from the entrance. "Did the little twerp make a friend?"

Ellio's stomach did a somersault. This was just about the time for Naruna's little collection racket. He'd been so consumed with thoughts of Kaya, it had completely slipped his mind. Ellio took a deep breath, trying to reign in his panic. Kaya was tough, but Naruna was vicious and insecure. If she gave the thug attitude, it could really set him off.

Thoughts raced through Ellio's mind. Kaya was proud. If she caught on to the fact that he was trying to protect her... Ellio gave an involuntary shudder.

Could he protect Kaya from Naruna, without her realizing what he was doing?

Ellio could see her studying him. Her brow furrowed as she took in his grimace, and she turned to look from him to the four men standing under the retractable repair-bay door.

The rusty metal slats had seen better days. Ellio couldn't even remember what color they were supposed to be. The paint had been swallowed up by rust, time, and the smog of the Downs. Naruna strutted through them like a king visiting one of his lowly vassals. Three cronies trailed in behind their boss.

If Ellio could get rid of Naruna quickly, maybe Kaya wouldn't figure it out. Or maybe he could play it off like he and Naruna were friends? Could he be that lucky? Kaya was many things, but unobservant wasn't one of them. Still, he had to do something.

Ellio stood and pasted a smile on his face. "H-Hey Naruna, good to see you." He waved an awkward hand in greeting before reaching down to help Kaya up. He half expected her to refuse, but she slid her warm, calloused palm across his with a slight smile.

Ellio saw Naruna's eyes widen as Kaya's slight form came into view. The gangster's thoughts were painfully obvious, transitioning quickly from shock to interest. Naruna's expression settled into a predatory gaze that Ellio didn't like one bit.

He was loath to leave Kaya's side, even for an instant, but there was one thing that might draw Naruna's attention away from a pretty face.

Ellio flung himself at the cabinet, tearing the door open and grabbing the entire cashbox in his haste. What did it matter if he lost a few extra coins? If he could distract Naruna and keep Kaya safe, it would be worth it.

"Here you go." Ellio jangled the cashbox in a way he hoped would entice the gangster. "I made some extra this week." In dismay, he noticed that Naruna was still fixated on Kaya. Even the money hadn't caught his attention.

"What's your hurry, twerp? You in a rush?" Naruna drawled. He raked his gaze down Kaya's body with a lewd grin. "It's almost like you don't want me around or something." The three thugs who had been lounging in the doorway perked up, as if awaiting a signal.

Ellio tried to laugh, but it came out more of a croak. "Of course not. I just know you're a busy guy..." He trailed off as Naruna waved an impatient hand at him, like he was an insect to be shooed away.

Taking a step closer to Kaya, Naruna peered down at her and crooned, "Where you from, little mouse? I coulda sworn I knew all the pretty faces 'round here."

Kaya raised her left eyebrow, giving Naruna a scornful look. She leaned around him to stare at Ellio. "Is this person your friend?" Her disapproval was obvious.

Ellio gripped the cashbox tightly to hide his shaking hands. "Not exactly. More of a neighborly acquaintance."

Naruna doubled over with laughter, clutching his stomach. "Friends with this grease monkey?" he roared. "You're a riot, sweet-cakes." He reached forward to swing a muscular arm around her shoulder, but she neatly slipped beyond his reach.

"I don't understand." Kaya looked back and forth between the young men.

Ellio tried to send her a reassuring smile, but it must have come out wrong because she took a step toward him, concern flooding her features.

"Ellio, what's—"

"It's all right," he interrupted desperately. Her movement jarred him into action. Ellio shook the cashbox like a maniac and somehow, miraculously, it caught Naruna's attention this time.

"Thanks, twerp." Naruna grabbed the box with a smirk. "Looks like this trash heap will be safe for another week." He tossed the box to one of the lackeys who trailed behind him. "Whaddaya say, angel face? I'll buy you a drink." He reached out for Kaya again and this time she smacked his hand away.

Ellio flinched and willed himself to keep calm. If he and Kaya could make it through a couple more seconds without incident, Naruna would lose interest. The gangster had a notoriously short attention span.

One of Naruna's cronies muttered from the doorway, "Is this chick stupid or something?"

"Ellio." Kaya put her hand on his shoulder. "Why are you giving him money?"

Ellio's face burned with shame. He hadn't considered what Kaya would think of him getting hustled right in front of her. He was going along with it today to keep her safe, but what about all the other times? He looked like such a loser. Ellio's shoulders slumped. "For protection," he muttered.

"*Accident* protection," Naruna snorted, laughing through his nose. "With a twerp like him, anything could happen." He kicked Ellio's tool chest, sending it slamming into the side wall. "See? Come on, sugar. I don't got all day. You gonna ditch this twerp or what?"

Kaya tugged on Ellio's sleeve, but he couldn't meet her eyes. It was over. Whatever slim thread of interest Kaya held for him must have snapped now that she knew how pathetic he really was.

He felt Kaya release his sleeve and turn toward Naruna. Ellio scrunched his eyes shut. He couldn't bear to see her walk away. Bile rose in his throat.

"I'll speak slowly and use small words so you can understand. Return Ellio's money and leave." Kaya's voice was low, almost soft. "*Now.*"

Warning trilled through Ellio's nerves, and he opened his eyes in alarm. When Kaya used that tone of voice, it meant trouble.

"This little mouse thinks she's a tiger." Naruna smirked over his shoulder to his goons. "Lucky for you, I like girls with a little bite."

He reached for her again and this time she stepped toward him, smiling. Knocking his arm aside, she struck his throat with the blade of her forearm. Naruna doubled over, coughing.

"That was a warning." She crossed her arms over her chest. "You're starting to annoy me."

"Kaya, no!" Ellio was horrified. He had to stop her before she made things worse. Clamping his hands around her left wrist, he tugged her toward him. "Please stay out of it. It's just the way things are. You don't understand."

"No, *you* don't understand." Her voice was steel as she jerked her wrist free from his grip.

Naruna stood, wheezing and clutching his throat. His face was mottled purple, and his eyes blazed. "You... stupid... skirt," he gasped between ragged breaths.

He lashed out at her with a sloppy fist, but Kaya was no longer there. She twirled around and kicked behind his knee. Naruna fell with a great crash.

Ellio couldn't tell who was more surprised, Naruna or himself. They stared at each other in mute shock as Naruna lay sprawled on the floor.

Ellio had always known Kaya was strong, but this... His thoughts were interrupted as Naruna lurched up, eyes bloodshot, spittle flecking his lips.

The gangster charged at Kaya. She stepped forward. Twisted her body into a punch that caught him across the face.

Naruna went down. Hands and knees slamming into the concrete floor. He spit out a wad of blood. Looked at it. With shaking fingers, he picked up a gold certa-dent and clenched it in his fist. "You're gonna pay for that!"

Gesturing wildly at his lackeys, Naruna bellowed, "What're you waiting for? Get her!"

Kaya's smile was feral, and she cracked her knuckles. "I was hoping you'd say that."

Stop, Kaya!

Ellio wanted to scream, but the words stuck in his throat. Naruna wouldn't hesitate to use violence. Even against a woman half his size.

He tried to wedge himself between Kaya and the entrance, but she slipped around him, heading straight for Naruna's three lackeys.

The three thugs were charging forward. Kaya ducked a fist thrown at her. Followed it up with a devastating uppercut. The thug went down like a sack of potatoes. Ellio could literally hear the breath knocked out of him.

The two other men were trying to box Kaya in. She smiled and darted forward toward the man on the left. Danced around his guard. Landed three precision strikes to his abdomen. The thug doubled over, gagging.

Naruna grabbed a wrench and swung it at Kaya's head. She swerved left. Came up behind him with an open palm strike behind his ear. Naruna went down hard. He didn't rise.

The last crony must have decided that Kaya wasn't worth it. But his maneuvering around the shop had put him within reach of Ellio. The thug swung a fist. Ellio stumbled, trying to get out of the way. Somehow, Kaya was there first. She knocked the fist aside with her forearm. Followed through with a ruthless elbow to the jaw.

Ellio winced at the crack. *That broke something.*

One of the thugs tried to throw the cashbox at Kaya's head, but she snatched it out of the air with ease. "Thank you." She curtsied at them as they swore, dragging their unconscious leader out of the shop.

The door slammed, freeing Ellio's tongue.

"What did you *do*?" he gasped.

Kaya turned to him, a look of fierce satisfaction on her face. Ellio noticed she wasn't even out of breath. She brushed off her hands and gave him a serious look. "Just taking out the trash."

"Are you serious?" Ellio exploded. "I had everything under control."

"Riiiiiight." She arched an eyebrow.

"I mean it, Kaya. Those guys are trouble. You have no idea what they're capable of."

She examined her nails for a moment and flicked a speck of lint off her sleeve. "They weren't capable of much."

"I was trying to distract them. If you could have just controlled yourself for a few more seconds—"

"Control myself? So, I should just let people rob you?"

"My priority was keeping you safe! Once they got what they wanted, they would have left."

Kaya snickered. "You. Keep me safe? From the likes of them? That's hilarious." She gave him a deadpan look.

"How was I supposed to know you were a martial arts prodigy? And where did you learn to fight like that, anyway?" Those movements were so familiar. Realization struck him like a thunderbolt. Ellio threw up his arms. "You're Silent Nyte!"

Her expression hardened, but she said nothing.

Ellio clutched his head. The storm of emotions warring in his mind made him dizzy. Silent Nyte, here in his shop! His heart skipped a beat remembering the light-purple flecks in her eyes. He had almost—but then Naruna had shown up. The happiness he felt for an instant was swallowed by gnawing darkness. "You lied to me." The accusation slipped through his lips in a bitter whisper.

"So what? People lie all the time." She crossed her arms and glared back.

Ellio chose not to take the bait. She wanted to twist the blame onto him. Kaya was upset he'd lied about Naruna. Disapproval radiated from her like a miniature sun. At least his intentions had been good. Who knew how many secrets Kaya was hiding from him? Clearing his throat, he tried to steer the conversation back onto her. "I thought you weren't allowed to leave the guild."

"We're not." She turned away from him, clenching her fists. "We're like birds in a gilded cage. Kept for the amusement of others."

Ellio flinched. Was she talking about him? Suddenly those Retiarius matches didn't seem so entertaining.

"No one knows I come here." Kaya's voice was quiet. "If they found out, there'd be consequences." Her back was to him, but he could see the tension in her body like a taut black thread. "I'll stop—"

"No!" The words burst from his mouth before his mind could catch up. "No, Kaya."

She turned back, a look of surprise etched on her face. Ellio reached forward and enveloped her in a bone-crunching hug.

"I don't want you to stop coming," Ellio whispered into the shell of her ear. "Please."

Kaya sighed, and he felt her small arms wrap around his waist. She nuzzled into the fabric of his jumpsuit. "Okay."

Ellio breathed in relief. It felt good to hold Kaya in his arms. Really good. She was warm and soft and seemed to fit perfectly against him. He tucked her head under his chin and grinned. He couldn't remember the last time he'd given anyone a hug.

He heard her mumble into his shoulder, "This is surprisingly pleasant."

Ellio laughed.

She squirmed, looking away. "You're not scared of me?"

His arms tightened around her for a moment and then he loosened his grip. Ellio pulled back slightly to grin down at her. "You're kidding, right? You've terrified me since the day we met. Remember the whole, 'If you're lying to me, I will break every bone in your body'?" The last part he spoke in a deep voice, scrunching his eyebrows in a parody of anger.

A blush swept across her cheeks, and she huffed, "What did you expect? I woke up in an unfamiliar place with a stranger snoring at my feet."

"I do not snore."

"Oh, yes, you do." She poked him in the chest, a grin starting to show through her frown. "Like a sagrin with a sinus infection."

Ellio spluttered in outrage for a moment before Kaya cupped his cheek in her palm. "Thank you for helping me that day." The laughter had disappeared from her eyes, her expression serious.

He grasped her hand and gave it a squeeze. "Of course." Just as he was working up the nerve to bend down a little closer, Kaya stepped away.

"I need to head back."

Ellio followed her to the door. "Will you be all right? Getting back, I mean."

Kaya turned to roll her eyes at him, a hand on her hip. "What do you think I am, an amateur?"

"Just be careful." Ellio leaned against the doorframe. It felt colder already, knowing she was leaving.

Kaya knocked him in the arm, but not hard enough to hurt. "I always am." And with that she slipped out of the shop without a backward glance.

Ellio sighed, watching her disappear around the corner. Things with Kaya were always more complicated than they appeared.

As Kaya took her normal route through the alleyways, she checked to make sure she wasn't being followed before slipping down a narrow street. There was a fire ladder in this alley. If she hopped, she could grab the bottom rung. Kaya climbed the ladder and hoisted herself onto the roof with ease. From here she could reach the guild with minimal scrutiny. The city of Beulah was a sprawling network of buildings. Houses, shops, and restaurants seemed to grow off each other like mushrooms, connected on the ground by patchwork streets, or vertically by bridges and rickety iron stairs. With street traffic being so jammed, many pedestrians made use of the bridges connecting buildings. But Kaya went even higher. Everyone was so absorbed in the drama of daily life, no one ever thought to look up and catch her moving along the rooftops.

As she prepared herself for the jump to the next landing, a tattered paper flyer stuck in the railing caught her eye. On it, gold letters curled invitingly around the following words:

Aurea Fall Festival

Traditional Booths and Games

Celebrate the Halyurite Meteor Shower with the one you love.

She examined the drawing of women in traditional Beulan robes. Fabric wrapped around their bodies in careful folds, dangling bobbles in their hair. Kaya traced her fingertip along the silhouette of a smiling woman holding hands with a young man.

The face of a blue-haired mechanic with golden eyes flickered through her mind. Kaya snorted, crumpled the paper into a ball, and tossed it off the roof.

I need to get a grip.

City of a Thousand Tears

KAYA TIPTOED TO THE door of Ellio's shop. It wasn't easy to be silent in the traditional wooden sandals she was wearing, but Kaya managed. Normally, she preferred boots or sturdy open-toed flats but today was a special occasion. She peered through the grubby window at her favorite blue-haired mechanic.

Ellio was leaning over his workbench, engrossed in a project. A thick electronics manual was spread open beside him, its pages creased with use. She watched as he counted on his fingers and then began scribbling furiously in a notepad. When he finished writing, Ellio rubbed his hands together and leaned forward over the table. Wires splayed out on both sides of him. Kaya watched him strip the wire casing off a set of blue strands and carefully twine them into a connector. Then he grabbed a metal panel beside him, fit it over the metal casing, and soldered it closed.

Kaya waited until she saw Ellio switch off the soldering iron before entering, taking care to jingle the bell attached to the door.

Ellio had pushed his goggles up into his hair and was admiring his work. "We're closed," he called out, not bothering to turn around.

He must be really excited about this project.

The thought made Kaya smile. She stepped further into the shop, deliberately making her shoes clack.

Ellio spun around on his stool and nearly dropped the piece of machinery he'd been working on. "Kaya!" The object almost slipped through his fumbling fingers a second time before he set it down on the workbench and sprang up to meet her. "You look amazing!"

Kaya smirked and did a little spin. She was wearing a traditional Beulan robe that fell to her ankles. The black satin fabric shimmered under the fluorescent lights, embellished with tiny purple-and-silver dragonflies. A delicate hairpin sparkled above her left ear, with little silver bells dangling from it. Kaya was particularly pleased with her eye makeup today. She'd managed to copy the shape of dragonfly wings in matching purple and silver. The wooden sandals gave her a few extra inches of height, all the better for spending time with Ellio.

She'd stashed the outfit in a safe house she'd prepared outside Retiarius and changed into it before coming to meet him. It had taken a lot of time and preparation but seeing the dazed expression on his face made it all worth it.

Kaya spread out her arms in a traditional Beulan pose. "You like it?"

"Like it? Are you kidding? You look incredible!" A blush spread across his face. Ellio headed toward her, and Kaya had the irrational hope that he would pick her up in his arms and spin her around. But then he stepped back, frowning.

"What are you doing here dressed like that? You're gonna get grease all over you," he fretted.

"It's black, Ellio," she huffed. "I'm not worried." Kaya put a hand on her hip and stuck out her lower lip. Why was he being so difficult? Wasn't he happy to see her?

Ellio fluttered around the shop, pushing drip pans out of the way, grabbing dirty rags and throwing them in the closet. He started wiping down his workbench, but in his haste, he knocked over a container of blue washer fluid. The liquid spread over the table and began dripping onto the floor.

"Aw, come on!" he groaned, throwing a cloth down.

Kaya watched him in confusion. What was going on? Ellio wasn't behaving like himself. This wasn't the reaction she'd anticipated.

A lightbulb went off in Kaya's mind.

He's nervous!

Strange. What did he have to be nervous about? Kaya puzzled over it for a moment. If Ellio was nervous, it was more likely he'd refuse her proposal. That wouldn't do. She needed to find a way to calm him down. Kaya drummed her fingers along her arm.

Of course! It was so simple.

Kaya clacked over to his workbench in her glossy black sandals.

"Be careful," Ellio warned. "It's a mess over here. I don't want to ruin your beautiful clothes."

"Don't worry about it." She waved his concerns away and tugged on his sleeve. "Tell me what you've been working on. It looks interesting."

Ellio's eyes brightened. "It's a new style of distributor I've been designing for the jetbike. By changing the input capacity, it'll allow a higher voltage through the engine. Of course, I'll have to modify the fusion plugs to compensate for that burst of power." He chatted happily, picking up the distributor to point out the modifications he'd made to the input ports.

It was impossible to curb Ellio's enthusiasm when talking about his inventions.

Kaya smiled at him and bumped her shoulder against his. "You know there's a festival today, right? Would you like to come with me? Retiarius lets us watch the parade from our balcony but that's it. Today I want to go."

"I don't know." Ellio swallowed and looked down. "I don't have the threads for anything like that. I doubt Aurea would let me through the gates." He shrugged with that deprecating half-smile of his.

Kaya put her hands on her hips. "I thought you might have a lame excuse like that. Which is why—"

She rummaged around her podpack for a moment before pulling out a rumpled shopping bag. With a flourish she lifted a beautiful scarlet robe from inside.

"I happened to come across this in one of my adventures last week. I think it'll fit."

She held the bag out to him, and Ellio blinked.

"For me? Are you sure?" His hands twitched, but he didn't reach out for the bag. A muscle in his jaw tightened. Ellio took a deep breath and looked away. "I don't know if I could repay you," he mumbled.

"It's a gift," Kaya answered firmly.

He still hesitated.

"Come on, Ellio. Live a little." Kaya waved the sleeve of the robe at him.

Ellio chuckled weakly and ran a hand through his hair, making it spikier than normal. At Kaya's pout, he held up his arms in defeat. "Okay," he conceded. "But I need a quick shower first. Make yourself at home for a few minutes."

Kaya nodded. As he slipped into the back room, she walked around to inspect the diagrams above his workbench. She was impressed by the amount of careful detail in Ellio's notes. Neat handwriting detailed different machine parts and their uses as well as mathematical equations to account for things like force, lift, and maglev capacity.

After a few minutes, she heard the shower in the other room turn off. There was a crash and the sound of bottles scattering, as if someone had bumped into a shelf and knocked over its contents. Ellio grumbled from inside and Kaya smiled. Although he was very detail-oriented, he could also be clumsy.

The door opened with a plume of steam and Kaya found herself peering curiously at the entrance. Ellio stepped out, scratching his neck, and Kaya's mouth popped open.

Sparkling clean from the shower, with his blue hair combed back, in the scarlet robe, Ellio was strikingly handsome. He didn't even have a smudge of grease on him—wait a minute. There was one.

"Bend down," Kaya commanded and when he complied, she wiped off a small streak that was hiding along the shadow of his jawline. "That's better. You look great, Ellio." She smiled at him and was strangely pleased by the blush tinting his cheeks. But then her eyes fell to the pair of black goggles strung around his neck. "You really love those goggles, don't you?"

"These?" He touched them with a smile. "They were my dad's. I must have put them back on again by reflex. I guess I don't really need them tonight." He slipped them over his head and placed them on top of a book on his workbench. "We don't have festivals in the Downs," he told her seriously. "So, I'm not sure what to expect."

"Then we'll find out together."

As the pair slipped out from the mechanic shop, Kaya's gaze flicked to a shadowed alley across the street. She could have sworn she saw movement, as a figure stepped further into the shadows. Kaya frowned and squinted her eyes, trying to see better. As the shadow had faded back into the darkness, the reflection of neon signs flashed briefly over the figure. Kaya thought she could just make out a glimpse of orange.

Ellio squeezed her hand. "Thanks for doing this, Kaya."

Suddenly, she felt very warm. Turning back to face him, Ellio's radiant smile made Kaya's heart stutter.

"Don't mention it," she murmured.

Why was she so flustered? Kaya shook her head. She was probably just riled up about sneaking out for the festival. It was a huge risk, but one glance at Ellio in his striking scarlet robe convinced Kaya it was worth it. Her nerves were making her paranoid, seeing things in the shadows that weren't there.

She steeled herself and squeezed Ellio's hand back. He ran his thumb over the back of her knuckles and a jolt of electricity ran through her. She cleared her throat. "C'mon, it's this way." She tugged his hand.

Kaya led him along the maze of streets, up narrow staircases, through tiny alleyways, and across rickety wooden bridges. She wove them deftly through the crowd, without ever letting go of Ellio's hand.

"You come all this way, just to see me?"

She turned back with a smile. "I like exploring."

"Yeah, I can see that."

After a long walk, they approached a grand stone staircase, and Ellio knew they'd passed out of the Downs. He'd noticed over the course of their walk that the people around him were becoming more well-dressed.

"Wow!" Ellio stared at the giant gates marking off Aurea district from the rest of the city. He hesitated and Kaya slipped her arm in his.

"Come on, Ellio."

He blushed and let her sweep him along. The gate guards didn't even give him a second glance. Inside Aurea was like another world. Shops didn't have cracked windows and smoke wasn't belching from the chimneys. The people were all dressed like Kaya, in beautiful robes and accessories. Ellio stopped to gape at his surroundings and someone bumped into him from behind. The girl tittered and batted her eyelashes at him. Normally an elegant girl like that would never give him the time of day. That's when he realized it.

I look just like them right now.

His thoughts were distracted by enormous red and gold balloons lifting off in the square.

"Kaya, look!" He tugged her closer. "That's awesome, using hot air! No maglevs at all."

A parade of dancers passed by, twirling colorful umbrellas and ribbons. They were followed by a passel of acrobats in red, doing flips and handstands, walking through the crowd.

Kaya smiled and let Ellio drag her over to a pair of jugglers. He nearly jumped out of his skin as the man next to them let out a big breath of fire! "Incredible!" He chuckled in wonder. "I never knew that Beulah had anything like this! It must be awesome to live in the golden district."

Kaya pursed her lips. A gust of smoky air blew their way and her eyes brightened. "I smell something sweet."

Ellio threaded his fingers through hers. He was taller and could see better in the crowd. "I think I see food stalls that way. Let's go."

At Kaya's eager nod, they headed in the direction of the sumptuous smell. Ellio got smoked fire squid on a stick. "This thing is enormous!" He gaped at the squid for a moment before digging in.

Kaya found a baker making delicious melon pies. She devoured hers in an instant. When Ellio offered to share his squid, she took a huge bite and then her eyes began to water.

"It's spicy!" She fanned her fingers in front of her face.

Ellio laughed. "Well, it *is* a fire squid."

After they found her some water, a booth caller's shout caught their attention. "Step right up and try your strength. The stronger you are, the bigger your prize!" He was standing beside a large pole with a bell rigged on top.

Kaya watched, tilting her head as a heavyset man approached with his family, his little daughter swinging on his arm. The caller gave the man a mallet, which he used to strike a pad beneath the pole. A little iron pellet ran up the pole with the force of his strike.

"Not bad, not bad," the caller cajoled, handing the man a small stuffed horse that he passed to his young daughter.

"Come on, Ellio. I want to try it." She tugged him over.

The caller beckoned to Ellio. "Hello, young man! Trying to win a prize for your girl?"

Ellio waved his hands in front of himself. "Not me. She wants to try." He jerked his thumb toward Kaya.

"This little lady?" The caller eyed her in surprise. "It's not really rigged for dames."

Kaya stepped forward with a grin, cracking her neck. She spat onto her hands and rubbed them together, grabbing the mallet from the aghast caller's hands. Taking a deep breath, she heaved the mallet over her head and slammed it down. The pellet shot up, ringing the bell loud and clear.

The caller gaped in shock but recovered quickly. "That's quite an arm you've got there, little lady," he said, laughing. "You've earned this." He gave her a giant stuffed panda.

"Way to go, Kaya!" Ellio cheered.

They laughed together at the sheer size of the stuffed animal. She glanced around for a moment, then spied the little girl with her father from earlier. "Here you go." Kaya nodded at her, waggling the panda's front paw.

The little girl's eyes grew wide, and she squealed with delight, clapping her hands. The panda was too big for her to carry, but her bewildered father took it in his arms as Kaya slipped quietly away.

"That was nice of you." Ellio smiled at her.

She looked down, nudging the gravel with the toe of her sandal.

A burst of trumpets split the air. Ellio and Kaya followed the sound. It was a parade. Masked dancers twirled ribbons streaming through the air; drums and cymbals rang out. They both laughed as tall men on stilts walked jauntily above the crowd.

"This is amazing!" Ellio breathed. "Hey, what's that over there?"

A crowd of people was gathered around a band. They were playing horns and stringed instruments while a catchy drumbeat had many people tapping their feet or nodding their heads. As Kaya and Ellio drifted closer, couples began to form, leaping and dancing joyfully.

"Would you like to try?" Ellio held out his hand to Kaya.

She hesitated. "I'm not sure how."

"I'm sure we'll be able to figure something out together." He grinned hopefully at her and his heart nearly burst through his chest as she placed her hand in his. As the music played, he spun her around. It was just as he thought. Kaya was a natural dancer; she twirled and glided as light as a feather. Dancing together they spun, dipped, dove, and twirled until the song ended and Kaya spun into him. Chests heaving, they grinned at each other in pure delight.

"See, we got this," Ellio said.

At that moment, two small children ran up to them, giggling.

"What are you doing?" Ellio chuckled as one child grabbed his hand and the other grabbed Kaya's. Before either of the young people knew it, the children had fastened a bright red string to each of their pinkies, connecting them. Then they ran away, still laughing.

"Wait," Ellio called after them, while Kaya stared down at the string, puzzled.

"It's for good luck," a merchant called out from his stall.

Ellio and Kaya walked over to his booth and asked him to explain.

"Red string of fate. Folks say it's good luck if you watch the meteor shower while attached to your true love. Try not to break it." The merchant waggled his eyebrows at Ellio with a wide grin.

Ellio felt like his cheeks were on fire. He gaped at the merchant for a moment before waving his hands frantically. "W-we're not..." he spluttered.

Kaya tugged on his sleeve. "It shouldn't be too hard to keep the string intact if we're careful."

"K-Kaya, did you hear what he said?" Ellio's voice warbled.

"He said it was good luck, didn't he?" She eyed the string connecting their two pinkies. "Let's try not to break it."

"Right," Ellio mumbled.

They continued browsing the stalls. Masks were very popular at this festival. Many people in the crowd were wearing them—princess masks, fox masks, toad masks. There were even some black demon masks strikingly similar to Silent Nyte's. Ellio eyed them with interest.

"Look, Kaya." He turned to tug on her sleeve and grab her attention, but Kaya suddenly threw herself at him and pulled them behind the stand. Her body was pressed up against his, her hands cinched around his right arm in a death grip. The red thread connecting their two pinkies twisted around itself as it dangled from her hand.

"Kaya, w-what—" he stuttered, and she clamped a hand over his mouth with a glare.

"There's another guild member," she whispered fiercely.

His eyes grew wide, and his brows drew down in a frown. "But I thought—"

"We're not supposed to be out on our own." Kaya nodded at him. "But she's here somehow." She edged around the side of the booth to have a quick peek. "Stiletto."

"No way! Stiletto's here? She used to be my favorite," Ellio said with excitement before Kaya slapped a hand over his mouth again with an annoyed look.

"We should be wearing masks too," she muttered.

Stiletto approached the mask stall, a red-and-white fox mask perched across her delicate nose. She pursed glossy red lips at the shopkeeper. "There was a young woman here a moment ago wearing a black robe. Did you see which way she went?"

Kaya took a quick peek beyond the stall then slunk further behind the booth, pulling Ellio with her. "We need to leave," she hissed. She jerked his arm toward a darkened alleyway but he resisted. The red string pulled taut between them, then snapped.

Ellio gasped in dismay, and Kaya turned back, eying the broken string.

"I..." She flexed her fingers, staring at the string still wound around her pinky. Then she shook her head. "There's no time!" She strode forward and grabbed his hand, tugging him toward a fire escape.

They rushed up the ladder and across a series of rooftops before Kaya let them rest.

"She almost caught us." Ellio wiped the sweat off his brow. "What would happen if Retiarius discovered you sneak out?"

Kaya fixed him with a piercing stare. "It wouldn't be good."

Stiletto was clearly still looking for them. It was easy to follow her brightly colored robe with all the lights from the festival. Ellio and Kaya shrank back from the edge of the roof. Kaya led him away up another series of ladders and rooftops until they were high enough to have a good view of the streets below and the night sky above.

"Do you think she saw us?"

"I don't think so. She'd still be following us."

"What's with her?"

"She... doesn't like me very much," Kaya admitted.

"Why?"

"I'm not sure. I just get that sense." Kaya stretched her hands above her head, and bent over backwards until her palms touched the floor. She popped back up again and Ellio laughed.

"Hey, you're pretty good. You've been here before, haven't you?"

"I like to come up here sometimes."

"All by yourself?"

She blinked and looked at him for a moment before turning to gaze at the sky. "Until today."

"Huh," Ellio whistled, then turned his gaze skyward. "Look at the stars, Kaya! You never see them like this in the Downs."

She smiled and sat beside him. "I like it here. It reminds me what it's like to be free."

"Free?" Ellio echoed.

"Yes." Kaya nodded. "In Retiarius, I'm just another prisoner."

Ellio felt his stomach churn. He hugged his arms around himself, squeezing. Kaya's admissions made him feel guilty. "I never knew that Retiarius was like that. In the Downs, we all thought Aureans had it so good."

"I don't blame you." Kaya shook her head. "It's what Retiarius wants people to think, the guild boss especially. Everyone here belongs to someone else. It's all a show."

"Beulah, City of a Thousand Tears," Ellio mumbled.

"What?"

"Beulah has a nickname in the Downs. She's called 'The City of a Thousand Tears.' She draws in the talented, the ambitious, the young. They all flock to her, hoping to make their fortune. Most end up in the Downs, destitute. The worst default on loans to the Heartless King. Then he sends in his reckoners to collect them. Drags them off to Gehenna till they've paid their debt. Beulah is a city built on broken dreams."

"The Heartless King," Kaya murmured. "To think Lucien's influence extends so far."

"I wouldn't be surprised if he owns half the city by now."

"Do you have a debt to Lucien?" Kaya's gaze was fixed on the floor.

"Nah, my dad never liked his vibe. We just used run-of-the-mill loan sharks."

Kaya's eyes widened. "You act like it's nothing."

Ellio laughed and ran a hand through his hair. "We've got all sorts in the Downs. Honestly, I try not to think about it much. But some day I wanna get out of here." His words came faster as he warmed to his topic. "I'm going to leave Beulah and travel, see the ocean."

"The ocean?" Kaya echoed.

"I've heard it's beautiful," Ellio gushed. She was watching him, head tilted to the side like a curious puppy. Noticing the intensity of her gaze drew a flash of heat up his neck. Oceans weren't the only things that were beautiful. Ellio cleared his throat. "But really, anywhere outside this city would be fine. I want to get as far away from Beulah as I can and never look back."

Kaya considered him for a moment. "You know, you remind me of my parents."

"Your parents?" Now it was Ellio's turn to eye her with interest.

"I try not to think about them most of the time." Kaya clenched her fists at her sides. "We used to live in Alsehir. My parents were sagrin herders, pacifists. But one day, bandits came. They raided our farm and killed everything. Didn't even bother eating the meat. Just killed them for sport. The poor, sad creatures had never known cruelty like that. My mother hid me. They murdered my parents on the sand. The bandits seemed to know a child was there, but they couldn't find me. Eventually they left. Probably thought I'd starve or get eaten by an ungalors that crept up from the desert."

Ellio covered her shaking fist with a warm hand. She let him gently pry open her fingers to squeeze her palm.

Kaya took a deep breath and continued. "Dragul found me in the desert and raised me. He taught me to read, write, how to survive. He brought me with him on his trading trips. While we were in Beulah the last time, we had a disagreement. I was angry. There was an incident. And I became indebted to the guild."

There was more to the story, but Kaya didn't speak it out loud. Dragul had seen something in her. Something that inspired him to teach her the fighting arts, but her explosive outbursts always upset him. She could still hear his lectures ringing in her ears.

A memory streaked across her mind.

Dragul's raspy voice had chided, "Your anger is holding you back."

"But I won!" Kaya protested.

"Anger can only get you so far. There will come a time when it's not enough."

Kaya huffed disparagingly. "Spare me the speech."

"Kaya, until you learn to control your anger, I refuse to teach you anymore." Dragul folded his arms across his chest.

"So that's it? You're just going to abandon me here?"

"When you're ready to continue the path of Eiren, seek me out. I'll be in Avathys."

Kaya punched the rock wall beside them. "You must be joking. Eiren? Don't tell me you're a believer like my foolish parents?"

"The warriors of Eiren are real, Kaya."

"They're fairy tales for weak-minded people."

"Your parents believed," Dragul reminded her.

"My parents were weak. And now they're dead."

"Kaya!" Dragul grabbed her shoulders and shook her.

"Forget it, I'm done." She slapped his hand away and stomped off down the street.

The memory skipped forward in time.

Kaya was eating in a tavern. She provoked a fight with a group of drunks, sending multiple people to med corp. As Beulah's enforcement squad detained her for processing, a Retiarius scout appeared and slipped a few coins into the inspector's hand.

"Why don't you let me have a moment alone with her first, Inspector?"

"Just a moment, then." The inspector turned away to his men.

Kaya's nails bit into her forearms as the memory concluded.

Ellio was studying her quietly.

She cleared her throat. "I couldn't refuse. It was Retiarius or jail. They paid off the enforcers, and now I'm working off my debt to them. I can't wait to get out of here."

"But you leave Retiarius all the time," Ellio pointed out. "You're here right now. Can't you just escape?"

Kaya shook her head. "Sneaking out for a few hours is one thing. If I disappeared when they had money on the line, it would be a different story. Tarak, the guild boss, would hunt me down to the ends of Elorah."

"Someday, let's leave Beulah together." Ellio grasped her hands. "We can go to the ocean."

"Now you definitely sound like my parents." Kaya chuckled. "Always dreaming. But no one is going to rescue us. There aren't any magical warriors of Eiren lurking in the shadows ready to pop out and save us. I would know; I'm on rooftops a lot."

"Did your parents talk about them?"

"Sometimes. They were like fairy stories that my mother would tell me before bed. Warriors of righteousness wreathed in blue flames, endowed with superhuman strength to do what was right, protect the weak and helpless. Those who couldn't defend themselves. When I think about it now, my mother spoke as if she really believed in them. It's strange, isn't it?"

"I don't think it's strange at all." He squeezed her hands in his. "Everyone wants to believe in something, don't they?" He swallowed, eyes falling to her lips.

Kaya followed his eye movement, leaning in closer.

His lips brushed against hers, warm and soft. The sensation was enthralling, intoxicating. Kaya wrapped her hands around Ellio's neck, wanting to pull him closer. He held her like she was made of glass. Like she could shatter in his arms. The irony of it made Kaya smile against his lips.

Ellio wants to protect me, she realized. For some reason the thought made warmth curl in her belly. She'd always thought being protected by others was a sign of weakness. But being around Ellio never made her feel weak. If anything, she felt stronger, more daring.

A distracted part of her mind knew they were missing the Halyurite meteor shower that streaked overhead. A once-in-a-lifetime view. Kaya silenced that little nagging voice, too caught up in Ellio's tender kiss.

Gathering Storm

Kaya tugged her robe closer around her shoulders. The night air was growing cold. She needed to hurry and lead Ellio back to the Downs. Clouds that had begun to gather during the festival darkened ominously.

Thunder rumbled overhead and rain came pouring down.

Ellio grabbed her hand and pulled her under a nearby awning. He peered upward with a frown. "Looks like this might last a while."

Kaya held out her hand, smiling as the drops dashed against her skin. "I've always loved the rain." She stepped out and spun around. "Come on, Ellio. It's refreshing."

Ellio eyed her from under the protection of the awning. "I seem to remember finding you, sick as a dog, out in the rain once."

Kaya huffed, hands on her hips. She drummed her fingers against her waist. Suddenly, her eyes lit up. She slipped off her sandals and looped her finger through the straps to carry them. "I'll race you."

"What?" Ellio laughed.

She pointed down the street to a shabby-looking clothing store. "To the next awning. I'll race you."

"We'll get soaked."

"What's the matter? Afraid you'll lose?"

"Probably." Ellio was smiling now.

"I'll give you a head start."

But Ellio was already running full sprint toward the clothing store. Kaya laughed and chased after him. Together, they ran from awning to awning along the street. Sometimes the awnings were full of holes and barely provided any cover from the rain. It developed into a game with both young people running madly through the Downs laughing, and careening off each other.

The rain got heavier, but they were enjoying themselves so much, they barely noticed. Ellio was just ahead of Kaya. He turned the last corner before his shop and stopped suddenly. So suddenly that Kaya bumped into him from behind.

"Ellio, you okay?" she asked.

His back was tense, and Kaya peered around him, frowning.

The door to his shop had been kicked in and hung from its hinges at a crooked angle. Kaya's smile died on her lips as the pair made their way silently toward the tattered "Aubri & Son" banner.

The windows were broken, shattered glass littering the floor. Pliers, screws, and oil canisters were scattered everywhere. His workbench had been flipped on its side, the wooden doors ripped off and obscenities carved into the paneling. Someone had gone through his toolbox and embedded all his wrenches in the drywall. Iridescent oil mixed with green antifreeze and red maglev solution, creating noxious-smelling whorls across the concrete. And there was a steady dripping coming from Ellio's precious jetbike. Kaya was no mechanic, but it looked like someone had taken a crowbar to the main compartment, tearing off hoses and denting the engine block. The brakes were stripped and hanging from the maglev boosters like misshapen party streamers. The utter destruction of the shop was further highlighted by the graffiti sprayed along the walls.

"Grease monkey."

"U R Nothin."

"100% loser."

Ellio stumbled into the room, eyes wide. He tripped over a maglev coil that had been stretched out of its spiral shape until it was almost unrecognizable. Kaya silently put her shoes back on, a grim mask pulled over her features as she took in the damage. This was a nightmare.

Ellio shuffled around in silence, rifling through the wads of paper and trash around his workbench, when suddenly he fell to his knees.

Kaya walked up behind him and peered over his shoulder. He was cradling his father's old goggles in his hands. One lens was missing, the other fractured with a spiderweb of cracks. The leather must have been sitting in a pool of bleach because the straps were now bleeding off their color like black tears. Ellio's hands were trembling.

"Ellio..."

"I told you to stay out of it," he whispered, yanking his shoulder away.

"What?" Kaya's voice came out higher than she would have liked. She squared her shoulders and marched around to face him.

"You should've just stayed out of it."

"What are you talking about?" She blinked, holding up her hands.

"With Naruna. Beating him up like that. Everything was fine before you got involved."

Kaya crossed her arms over her chest and glared at him. "Are you kidding? What was I supposed to do, let him rob you?"

Ellio let out a bitter laugh. Kaya had never heard his voice take a tone like that before. "That's how life is in the Downs."

"I don't accept that." She shook her head, putting her hands on her hips. "People like him will walk all over you unless you confront them."

Ellio stood and looked down at her, hands balled into fists, eyes blazing. "But I didn't confront him. *You* did. You made the choice for me. And look where it got me! He's destroyed my shop. It probably didn't look like much to you, but it was all I had, Kaya. It was everything I had left of my father."

"Clean it up and get over it." Internally, Kaya winced. She'd crossed a line, but the words poured out of her. "At least you have something to remember your father by. I have nothing." She gestured around the shop with a sweeping arm. "Besides, the damage is minimal. Those jerks only went for the obvious stuff. It won't take long to fix..." She was going to add, "We can do it together," but seeing Ellio's furious expression, the words died in her throat.

He was still glaring at her, and Kaya had never seen his face contorted in anger like that. "I don't expect you to understand." Ellio's voice was acerbic. "An Aurean like you who goes to festivals, buys designer clothes, and has everything handed to her."

"Don't push me, Ellio!" Kaya leaned forward and jabbed her finger into his chest. "You have no idea what you're talking about. I'm like a princess from some cliché, held in the highest room in the tallest tower. I can't even walk down the street without constantly watching my back."

"Poor Kaya. You're right, you've really had it rough." He rolled his eyes at her.

Kaya could feel her blood starting to boil. She took a deep breath trying to calm down, but his mocking expression drew the words out of her like poison.

"This happened because you're a coward. Because you're too weak to fight back. Why don't you get some pride, for Dral's sake? You could leave this place if you had the courage. If you stopped doing repairs in exchange for stale noodles and muffins. Grow up."

Lightning flashed through the sky, and the shop was illuminated for a moment. The thunder followed close behind; its deep echo shook the walls. Ellio let his father's goggles slip through his fingers and fall to the floor. He turned away from her, hands shaking against his sides. "Why do you bother coming here?" he muttered.

"Excuse me?"

"You heard me. If I'm such a pathetic loser, why do you keep coming around?"

"I never said—"

Ellio whirled around and took a step toward her, throwing his hands in the air. "Did you think a stupid robe was magically going to fix everything? It doesn't matter what I wear, Kaya. I'm always going to be a gutter rat with no future. Maybe you can't accept that, but I can. Stop ruining my life with your spoiled little tantrums!"

She wanted to punch him. Her fists tingled with fury, and her lips curled back in a snarl.

He laughed, eyeing her trembling form. "That's all you're good for, isn't it? Hurting people."

Kaya took a shaky breath. How did things get out of control so fast? She didn't want to fight with Ellio, she realized in surprise. Somehow, she wanted to make things right. Kaya breathed through her nose, willing herself to stay calm.

Ellio shifted his stance, exaggerating the height difference between them. He looked down at her, scorn hardening the planes of his face.

Something inside her snapped like a wire wound too tight. The words popped out of her mouth before she could stop them. "I'm not gonna let you blame me for everything. Maybe it's a good thing your old man's gone. Seeing you cower like a kicked dog would've made him die of shame." Nausea followed the words up her throat. Her stomach clenched like she'd just taken a fist to the gut. Kaya stifled the urge to clamp a hand over her mouth.

Ellio turned away again, his shoulders slumped. "Just get out," he muttered.

Kaya couldn't stop herself from taunting, "What was that, Ellio? Speak up."

"I said, get out!" Ellio roared. "Stop coming around here." He kicked a paint can across the room. It splattered against the wall, leaving a dripping red slash.

Kaya felt something start to crumble in her chest. Instantly, the instinct to fight was gone, swallowed by a suffocating dread. The words had gotten all twisted somewhere between her heart and her throat. Why couldn't he understand? She didn't mean it.

"Ellio..."

"I *never* want to see you again."

The finality of his words tore through her. It reminded her of another conversation. When Dragul refused to continue her training. Before she had smashed her way through a Beulan tavern and gotten ensnared by Retiarius.

What was it Dragul had said? Something about needing to control her temper. The words were different, but the feeling of loss was the same.

A bitter taste seared her throat. "Fine." Kaya turned on her heel and stomped toward the door. Stepping over the wooden fragments, she put a hand on the door frame and glanced back. Ellio had turned away. He bent down and began picking up screws and bolts that had scattered from his tool chest. Kaya slipped out into the night.

She had forgotten it was raining. A gust of wind sliced through her wet clothes, making her shiver. She turned her face to the sky. The smog from the Downs always made it too hazy to see the stars, but she tried anyway. Raindrops streaked down her face. Kaya swiped at her cheek with the back of her hand and frowned. Makeup smudged her hand like she'd been crying tears of silver and purple.

She looked back once more through the doorway of Ellio's shop, but he had moved out of sight. Her skin prickled. If he didn't want her here, fine. She was happy to leave. Head held high, Kaya stormed out into the street, heedless of the cold.

Her feet were lead weights, growing heavier with every step. She realized she was wandering aimlessly, not taking her usual route, not taking any of her precautions to avoid being followed.

A vision of Ellio's face swam into her mind, and she remembered how he'd looked at her, the anger fading from his eyes into a cold, hard indifference. Like he'd cut her out of his heart.

Kaya slammed her fist into a nearby dumpster, leaving a dent. Pain shot up her wrist. She pulled back her fist and massaged the knuckles with her right hand.

That's when she heard a chuckle.

"Now, now, we don't want you damaging those beautiful hands before your next match, Kaya."

She turned toward the voice, body tense, berating herself for not paying better attention.

Eight trackers were closing in on her. Four coming up one side of the street and four moving in from behind. Retiarius had caught onto her. Kaya was willing to bet they also had eyes on the roof and a clanker containment vehicle around the corner. This wasn't a great place to make a stand, but she'd have to try.

Ellio...

Her thoughts veered again toward the blue-haired mechanic with golden-brown eyes and kisses that made her come alive. Kaya gritted her teeth and shook her head.

I can't afford distractions.

She kicked off her shoes and opened her bare feet into a fighting stance.

Ellio groaned. He'd been picking through the tools scattered around his shop, but his mind was reeling, his thoughts a tangled snarl of anger and remorse. Stooping down, he examined a ratchet wrench with bent prongs. Hopeless. The wrench was a goner. He put it to the side in a pile of mangled tools. Later he'd carry it out to the dumpster.

Stop thinking about her.

Ellio turned and couldn't stop his eyes from drifting to his cot. The frame was twisted in half. He stood and walked over to it. Picking it up, he attempted to straighten the frame when he saw his blanket crumpled on the floor beside it. Oil was soaking into the corner, creating a large brown stain.

Unbidden, a memory of Kaya flashed through his mind. He remembered when she was sick and had lain on his cot, his blanket tucked under her chin. He remembered placing the damp rag across her forehead.

Ellio shook his head. He didn't want to think of her; he needed to focus. Leaving the cot for now, he turned toward his workbench and strained to tilt it upright. Tools and bits of wiring scattered, and his Zenon burner rolled away, the port crumpled.

Again, he remembered Kaya leaning around him as he stirred a pot of Melty O's. She was sniffing the steam with her eyes closed, a hint of a smile shining through her normally reserved expression. She opened her eyes and a light blush dusted her cheeks as she met his gaze. Ellio remembered how he had gotten lost in that look. Distracted by the beautiful violet color of her eyes, he'd let the Melty O's get slightly scorched. He remembered her pout as she crunched on the burnt porridge, nose wrinkling.

Ellio kicked the Zenon burner, and it went flying against the wall, spraying lighter fluid around it like a halo.

She's antagonistic. She's violent. She's got zero empathy or compassion.

But she'd been so delighted when the little girl tied the red string to her pinky. He looked down at his hand. The thread was broken, but a little scrap still dangled from his finger.

"You're a dreamer, like my parents." He remembered her voice. He remembered kissing her on the rooftop. The feeling that bloomed in his chest like a fire.

I don't want to lose that! I don't want to lose her.

Ellio sprang up, dropping the handful of screws. He ran toward the door, tripping over a broken drawer. Ellio stumbled but didn't fall. Running into the rain, he held a hand over his brow, trying to see which way she could have gone. Lightning tore through the sky overhead.

"Kaya!" he shouted. It was impossible. How could he hope to find her when she didn't want to be found? He headed toward the route she had brought him. Two alleyways down on the right was the route she'd taken to bring him to Aurea.

As he made his way there, he heard a commotion. People shouting. A body flew out of the alleyway and skidded down the street.

Kaya's handiwork; Ellio was sure of it.

The man, dressed in a black suit with black gloves, picked himself up and ran back toward the alley, flipping the protective shield of his combat visor over his face.

Ellio raced after him and peered around the corner. The sight stopped him in his tracks.

Kaya was fighting eight grown men. The seam of her robe was torn open to the thigh, and she flailed out at her attackers with a flurry of kicks and punches.

She's amazing.

Ellio gaped, watching her blows flow like water.

"Really, Kaya," one of the men spoke out. The others halted at his words. "I was hoping you'd come back without making a scene. But after your disaster at the tavern, I'm not surprised. You never knew how to pick your battles." The man gave Kaya a nasty smirk and motioned to the other guards.

They had her surrounded.

Kaya squared off against them. She wasn't going down without a fight. Then Ellio's face flashed into her mind. She saw a vision of him turning away from her. "I *never* want to see you again," the specter hissed.

Kaya stumbled. The Retiarius guards were on her in an instant. They wrestled her to the floor. Still, she fought. Ellio watched her whip out with an elbow and give one man a blow that was sure to leave a black eye in the morning. But they overpowered her, pushed her down into a muddy puddle, and clamped magcuffs onto her wrists.

Ellio froze. Sweat trickled down the back of his neck. His heart threw itself against his ribcage as he watched the lead guard bring out a horrific-looking collar.

"Nobody leaves the guild, Kaya. It's time you learned that." The guard held up the device, its metal edge reflecting the gleam of the streetlamp.

Kaya tried to jerk herself free, and the man smiled at her efforts.

"So, you recognize this?" He twirled the collar with his finger. "A bio-collar coded to Tarak himself. It won't release without his personal DNA signature. One step outside the compound and you'll be zapped within an inch of your life. I can activate it at any time, but if you're a good little girl, I'll wait until we've passed through the gate."

Six of the guards were holding her down, but Kaya broke free and lunged at the man.

He signaled to the other guards, and they forced Kaya back to her knees. Then he leaned forward and snapped the collar around her neck. "You won't be escaping again, I promise you."

Kaya glared at the man but didn't reply. She still managed to look defiant, despite her dirt-smudged face and torn clothes.

One of the guards brought the clanker around and they shoved Kaya in, headfirst, the rest of the guildsmen pouring in after her.

The slam of the door shattered Ellio from his inertia. He rushed forward, but the clanker was already moving, turning the corner into a busy street. Ellio sprinted after it.

How could this happen? She always covered her trail. But Retiarius had discovered her and now they'd be extra cautious. Biometric collars were said to be uncrackable.

And she'd think he meant all those things stupid things he'd said.

What have I done?

Ellio wrenched his hands in his hair and screamed into the night.

"Kaya!"

Breaking Point

Rain splattered against the window of the clanker. Kaya stared out, feeling numb. She should be concerned with the confrontation she knew was coming. Guild boss Tarak would be waiting for her when they got back to Retiarius. She watched the people moving outside the rain-streaked window. The world seemed like a black-and-white movie, with everyone moving in slow motion.

Getting caught should have bothered her, but she couldn't bring herself to care. Ellio's face, the look of pain twisting his features, played on repeat in her mind. And his voice, so broken and disheartened, telling her to go away.

He didn't want to see her anymore.

The pain this caused wasn't new to Kaya. There was no physical reason for the tightness in her chest. Like a giant fist had squeezed all the air from her lungs. She barely felt it when the guards jerked her roughly out of the vehicle and shoved her up the stairs. Retiarius's grand entrance had a lot of stairs, the ornate golden rails curling around sculptures of acrobatic fighters, flowers, and leaves.

Soon she found herself pushed into Tarak's office and the door snicked closed behind her. Kaya stood, dripping wet in her torn robe. She put on an arrogant sneer as the guild boss turned from the window to face her.

Tarak was tall and broad-shouldered. He probably could have been a fighter himself, but his true strength lay in his ability to manipulate and coerce from the shadows. He puffed on a thick cigar. The smoke stung Kaya's nostrils, but she refused to show her discomfort. Dragul had trained her well. At the memory of her old mentor, Kaya's mouth twisted into a scowl.

"You've caused me a good deal of trouble, little bird." Tarak's voice was raspy from a lifetime of cigar smoke. "Imagine my surprise when I received a call from the Downs, telling me one of my chicks had strayed from the nest. It makes me look bad, Kaya." He ground his cigar in the stone ashtray on his desk. "You don't want to tarnish my reputation, do you?"

Kaya stared at him coolly, not saying a word. She brought her cuffed hands to her face and flicked her bangs away from her eye with a pinky.

"And don't think you can hide your little dalliances with that grimy mechanic either."

At this, Kaya's eyes flashed. She met his gaze unwillingly before looking away.

"Struck a nerve, did I? I know all about the Aubri boy. Though I'm surprised your standards are so low. I always thought you had more refined taste."

She tried to lunge forward but found herself restrained by the magcuffs on her wrists. Tarak must have installed a metal plate under the rug. The invisible magnetic field it generated wouldn't allow her to move beyond its boundary until he deactivated it. He raised an eyebrow at her, unimpressed.

"You have proven unexpectedly resourceful. But you're still a valuable asset to me. A diamond in the rough, so to speak. You're going to make me millions and you're going to do it quietly and obediently from now on, little bird. No more nightly escapades. Do I make myself clear?"

Kaya scoffed and made a rude hand gesture.

"I don't think you understand, so let me elaborate. You're too valuable for me to dole out my usual punishments. If you can't fight, you're no use to me. This forces me to be a little more creative." He strolled around to the front of his desk and leaned back against it, elbows against the polished ruewood. "People in the Downs go missing all the time. They're like rats. I doubt anyone would notice the disappearance of one pitiful mechanic."

Kaya's skin prickled, hair rising on the back of her neck. She repressed a shudder.

Tarak leaned toward her, so close she could see the tobacco stains on his teeth. "Let me be clear. I've killed important and powerful people to get where I am today. I would have no problem eliminating that boy."

Kaya flinched as if his words were a slap. Real fear flooded her eyes for the first time and her sneer bled off her face like ink.

Tarak laughed. "I found the right button to push, didn't I, little bird?"

Kaya pressed her lips together. If Tarak knew about Ellio and considered him a threat, it would be easy for the guild boss to have him killed. "I'll behave," she ground out.

"Good. I think we understand one another." Tarak leaned forward and tousled her wet hair. "It goes without saying, his life will be forfeit the minute you have any further contact."

Kaya's lips curled back into a snarl and the guild boss stepped back.

He pushed a button on his desk, calling for his guards. With a wave of his hand, he gestured for them to take Kaya away, deactivating the magnetic field so that she could move beyond the carpet.

The guards thrust Kaya back into her room and she gave a start. Thick iron bars had been welded in a grid pattern across her window. Tarak wasn't taking any chances. She sank onto the mattress, hands in her lap. After a few moments the magcuffs blinked and shut off. They fell from her wrists and she shoved them onto the floor, kicking them away. Tarak had probably made other modifications to her room to keep her prisoner. At least until her body was broken and beyond use to Retiarius.

Kaya walked to the window and looked out. She saw small motion detector nodes along the edges. Gazing out at the night sky, Kaya's shoulders sagged. The moon and stars were completely swallowed up in a cloudy haze. She wouldn't be able to derive any comfort from them tonight.

Ellio...

Her heart twisted like a knife in her chest.

He'll think I don't care, that I don't want to see him.

Tarak's threat burned hotter than a brand on her skin.

And there's no way for me to tell him the truth, because Tarak will have him killed.

A tear trickled down her cheek as she pressed her forehead against the iron bars.

Ellio rounded the corner and watched the clanker disappear into the snarl of traffic. There was no way he'd be able to follow it on foot. Lightning flashed overhead. Rain soaked through his shirt, until it stuck to his skin. Ellio sloshed through a puddle, the muddy water squelching into his boots. But he hardly noticed. He shambled back to his shop in a fugue of despair.

Kaya, you're farther away than ever.

This time it wasn't just money or social class separating them. The guild boss was personally involved.

A bio collar linked to Tarak himself. Not even Kaya will be able to get around that.

Ellio stumbled into the shadowy mechanic shop. The lights flickered overhead. Two were broken, casting his shop in pale spots of fluorescence.

I just stood there like an idiot and let them take her.

Ellio ground his fists against his temples with a groan. How could he have been so stupid? He should have done something, anything! Ellio kicked a pile of maglev coils. He picked up a torque wrench and threw it against the wall.

I'm such a coward!

But what could he have done? Not even Kaya stood a chance against all those guards.

Everything reminded him of her. How she used to read on his cot, legs dangling off the edge as he repaired the sling loader. How she laughed at his off-tune humming while he worked. How she always wanted to eat Melty O's but would never admit it. Her insatiable sweet tooth.

All I can do is fix machines. I can't help real people.

Ellio roared in frustration. He was tired of feeling helpless.

A dripping sound made him turn his head. The jetbike was leaking oil like a sieve. The sight of his broken bike filled him with fury. Ellio flung himself at the machine and tore at the cables. He yanked off the side-view mirror and hurled it over his shoulder. His pulse raged in his ears, and he started kicking his jetbike in time with the beat, cursing.

Behind him came a snarky laugh.

"You losing it or something?"

Naruna.

Ellio stopped kicking but didn't turn around. His breath came in great, heaving gasps. His hands were shaking. Sweat stung his eyes.

He could hear Naruna picking his way through the debris on the floor. The thug hated to be ignored. Ellio took a deep breath in through his nose. He really wasn't in the mood.

Naruna sauntered close, mocking. "So, the little mouse stopped slumming? Or did Retiarius pick her up?"

A surge of anger flooded Ellio's veins like molten lead. "What did you say?"

Naruna slung an arm around Ellio's neck, knuckling his head. "Did you really think we wouldn't notice? That chick's got Retiarius written all over her. And we all know they're not supposed to go wandering around alone, 'specially in the Downs."

Ellio twisted out from under his arm, fist swinging.

The blow caught Naruna on the side of the jaw, whipping his head back. He stumbled a few steps, then caught his balance, mouth gaping.

Naruna stared at Ellio in disbelief. Then he reached up and wiped the back of his nose with a dry chuckle. "Finally found something worth fighting for? About time, loser."

Ellio threw himself at Naruna and the two went tumbling to the ground. Naruna was strong, but Ellio was in a rage. They rolled across the floor, grabbing, punching, screaming.

Naruna wrenched himself free and both young men staggered to their feet, chests heaving.

The thug lunged toward a pile of tools and snatched a large metal socket wrench.

Ellio's eyes darted around the shop.

There!

His fingers closed around the handle of his blowtorch. He clicked it on, and the bright-blue flame rumbled to life.

Naruna froze, eyes wide.

Ellio held up his free hand, palm out. "We used to be friends, Naruna. What happened?"

Naruna's stillness was unnatural. Almost like he was made of stone. He licked his lips, studying Ellio. His eyes narrowed, and he seemed to make a decision. Slowly, he bent down and placed the wrench on the floor.

"Never thought you'd have the guts," Naruna muttered. Then rousing himself, he spoke louder. "You piss me off."

"Why?" Ellio demanded. "I've never done anything to you."

"If you haven't figured it out by now, you're not gonna," Naruna huffed. "People talk like you're some kinda genius, but you haven't got a clue."

Confusion swirled in Ellio's mind. What did Naruna have against him? He took a step forward, still holding the blowtorch and Naruna flinched.

Realization shot up Ellio's spine.

The bruises. The burn marks. That time Naruna came out to play, limping, his two front teeth gone. "I fell," was all he'd say.

But Naruna never fell when they played together as kids. He wasn't clumsy.

Ellio swallowed. His heart twisted in his chest as he took in Naruna's pained expression. It felt like a bucket of lug nuts had been poured down his throat. "Naruna."

"Will you put that stupid thing away?" Naruna gestured toward the blowtorch, his gaze flitting around the shop. He wouldn't look Ellio in the eye.

Ellio searched his memory. Naruna's dad was a hazy figure in his mind. Wreathed in shadows and alcohol fumes, he hadn't been around much when they were kids. Naruna never talked about him.

Ellio frowned and set down the blowtorch. "When we were kids—"

"Shut up," Naruna interrupted, flinging out a hand as if to stop Ellio's words. "Last thing I want's a trip down memory lane with *you*." He dragged a hand over his cropped hair.

"But your dad—"

"I said *SHUT UP!*" Naruna brayed, voice cracking. His body trembled.

Naruna was a mess. Eyes bloodshot, lip split open, chest heaving. Scraps of paper stuck to his legs, oil stains splattered across his chest. He looked like he'd been run over by a street sweeper.

"You're weak and useless, but people've always liked you better. What's so great about you, huh?" He waved a hand dismissively in Ellio's direction.

"I..." Ellio swallowed. He shifted his feet and looked at the floor.

"You stay nice and safe in your little shop, letting other people fight for you. You think hiding in here makes you better than me? Just makes you gutless!"

"What am I supposed to do?" Ellio yelled, throwing up his hands. "Be a criminal? *That's* your answer?"

"Do something!" Naruna hollered. "Do anything! Besides wasting your life in the Downs." His voice grew quiet. "You're not like the rest of us. You got something different. And I'm tired of watching you throw it away."

One of his cronies poked his head around the door. "Everything okay, boss?"

"Yeah," Naruna drawled. "We're leaving." He waved his lackey back outside and looked at Ellio once more.

Ellio swallowed. He had to get this out before Naruna left. "I'm sorry... about what happened with your dad. I didn't know."

Naruna tried to laugh, but it almost sounded like a sob. "Don't matter. I settled the score a long time ago." His eyes flicked toward Ellio, studying him. "Your pops found me that day. The day my old man knocked out my teeth." Naruna's voice was quiet. His hand drifted toward his mouth before he clenched it tightly to his side. "Aubri cleaned me up. Gave me a pep talk. Inspired these babies." He smirked and pointed to his reinstalled certa-dents.

"They're, ah, shiny," Ellio fumbled.

Naruna snorted. "Drove me crazy you had such a great pops, when mine was..." He struggled to find the word then gave up with a shrug. "Outta respect for Aubri, I'm not gonna pound you into the ground for that punch. It was sloppy, but not a total loss. Maybe you got some backbone after all." He rubbed his jaw, then smirked and headed toward the door. He grabbed the handle and looked back, face serious. "I know you like her, but don't do something stupid. Retiarius is another level. You mess with them, you're gonna get yourself killed."

As Naruna stepped outside, Ellio's adrenaline started to wane. He slumped against a wall and slid to the floor.

Mess with Retiarius? He wasn't crazy.

Ellio sighed and rubbed his temples. But the more he thought about it, the more the idea stuck. He'd confronted Naruna; something he'd fantasized about forever.

What if rescuing Kaya wasn't impossible?

He couldn't fight. Even getting the drop on Naruna, the thug had still managed to get quite a few hits of his own. Ellio would have bruises tomorrow.

But what he lacked in physical strength, he made up for with machines. Why couldn't he use tech to break Kaya out? Even that bio-collar must have a power source. With the right electromagnetic pulse, he could short-circuit it.

I could fit it in a wristwatch.

But how could he find Kaya? Retiarius was huge. Then he recalled her words. *I'm like a princess locked away in the highest room of the tallest tower.*

Was she being dramatic?

Ellio shook his head. Kaya had spoken of watching the stars from her tower window during her visits. She *did* have a room high in Retiarius's tower.

Could he break into the heavily fortified guild? He'd need a distraction. Maybe a power outage? Then disengage the security systems. And find a way to get out again.

Ellio looked at his broken jetbike, mind humming. He smiled, remembering Naruna. It wasn't like they were friends, but Naruna's words implied a grudging respect. Like he'd proven his worth—if only a little.

"Sorry, Naruna," he whispered. "Looks like I'm about to do something stupid."

Ellio grinned and pulled his goggles over his eyes. Time to get to work.

Supernova

"Silent Nyte still isn't appearing in any matches." Tanyi, a bright-faced novice, slid into the seat across from Stiletto in the dining hall.

Retiarius spared no expense on its appearance. The hall had a beautiful vaulted ceiling and marble floors. Statues of previous champions were meticulously carved and posed gloriously in the alcoves, lit by soft mood lights. Legendary fighters like Black Wing, Fiamma, and Sanctus gazed down at the fledgling trainees, inspiring them to greatness.

Stiletto lounged in her chair, bored. Nothing interesting had happened lately. Kaya appeared to be under lock and key, and without her nemesis to stalk, things just weren't as exciting.

Tanyi leaned across the table, whispering in a conspiratorial way, "If this keeps up, you'll win Fighter of the Year for sure."

Stiletto's eyes slid to the girl and Tanyi moved back. There was something vicious in the brunette's gaze.

"You'd better watch your tongue, Tanyi. Before someone cuts it out." Stiletto gave her a cruel smile.

Tanyi gulped and bowed her head. She picked up her tray and moved further down the table.

This isn't what I wanted, Stiletto mused to herself. *Winning like this isn't satisfying at all. It didn't matter how I eliminated the other girls, but Kaya, she's different.*

Stiletto twirled her knife in her hand and flung it at the wall. It stuck, piercing an ancient tapestry of water nymphs playing around a fountain.

Kaya was so quiet, so indifferent to the cheers of the guild. She didn't care about the fans; she only cared about winning.

So distant, so arrogant. Always acting like she was above the rest of us. But look at you now, Kaya.

Stiletto toyed with the buckwheat noodles in her bowl.

I wanted to wipe that smug expression off her face. To see her suffer. It's gotta be combat or nothing at all.

A storm was coming. Stiletto was going to make sure of that. She stood, ready to go to her room and plan.

The light bulbs buzzed overhead. All at once they grew blindly bright and then exploded with a loud bang. Shattered glass rained down on the girls and screams split the air.

Ellio blinked and jumped back as sparks leaped from the fuse box. One caught on the fabric of his sleeve, and he hastily patted it out. He'd meant for the blast box to force the power system into an emergency shutdown and reboot. But it seemed he'd misjudged the strength of the burst. It had created an electrical overload, burned through the circuits, and caused a surge of power that fried everything connected to it.

A distraction's a distraction, right?

He keyed a code into the digital control panel strapped to his wrist and remotely activated his jetbike. It floated forward, maglev coils humming. Ellio slung his leg over the seat and initiated altitude gain, aiming for the tower.

Kaya, I'm coming!

He spiraled around the tower until he got to the level of the windows just below the roof. One of them had thick iron bars welded across it.

I bet that's where she is.

He saw the flash of red emergency lighting activating inside. Their backup generators had already kicked in. He needed to find her before the security net could reboot.

"Kaya!" He banged on the glass. "Kaya, are you in there?"

He saw a shadowy form run to the window and throw the glass open.

"Ellio!" It was Kaya. Her voice cracked in disbelief. She reached through the bars, and he kissed her fingertips. She pulled back her hand with a squeak, then demanded, "What are you doing here?"

"Rescuing you." He puffed out his chest and struck a dashing pose on his jetbike.

"Are you insane? If they catch you—"

"Then let's not get caught." He lowered his goggles and held out a sticky det charge. "Stand back."

Kaya backed away and Ellio carefully placed a ring of charges around the window. He moved the jetbike back a few meters and activated the fuse with his control panel. The window blew out, bricks around it crumbling from the wall, leaving a gaping hole in its wake.

Ellio pulled up to the opening and leaped into Kaya's room.

She threw herself into his arms. "I thought you didn't want to see me anymore," she mumbled into his chest.

He wrapped his around her, and bent to whisper into her ear. "I'm sorry. I didn't mean it. When I saw them taking you away—"

"You saw?" Her voice was sharp.

"The Retiarius guards? Yeah, I saw you fighting. You were incredible."

Kaya sagged against him. "Not good enough." She reached out with her hand and cupped his cheek. "I thought I'd never see you again," she whispered.

Ellio chuckled. "You can't get rid of Downsians that easily. We're like barnacles—"

His words were cut off as Kaya grabbed a fistful of his collar and crushed her lips to his. Ellio tightened his arms around her slim waist, tugging her closer. It was so easy to get lost in her.

A warning alarm beeped on his control panel, and he pulled away reluctantly. "As much as I'd like to continue, we need to go."

Kaya tugged on the bio collar. "But this stupid thing—"

"Really, Kaya. What do you take me for?" Ellio fiddled with his wrist-watch. "I just need a minute. This micro-pulse generator should disrupt the collar's power source long enough for me to remove it."

Kaya's eyes sparkled, and she looked at him in awe. "You're amazing, you know that?"

The corner of Ellio's mouth quirked up into a smile. "I could stand to hear that more often." He adjusted the knobs on the watch, biting his lip. "Almost there—"

Kaya's bedroom door burst open. A smoke grenade spiraled through the air, exploding at their feet. They could hear the shouts of guards outside. A burst of tranquilizer darts shot through the open door. Kaya took a protective stance in front of Ellio.

"Everything good back there?" she called out.

He stumbled and leaned against the wall. Between the smoke and the red emergency lighting, he could barely make out Kaya's silhouette. His legs felt like they were made of jelly. A tingling sensation spread down his limbs. Ellio pulled a tranq dart from his shoulder and looked at it curiously.

"Yeah... sure," he muttered, letting it slip through his fingers. "All... good." He blinked, trying to focus, but the room was spinning. Ellio could hear Kaya shouting. The world tilted sideways; darkness seeped through the corners of his vision.

And then, everything went black.

Icy water splashed in Ellio's face and he jerked awake. Groaning, he tried to reach for his aching head, only to find he was strapped to a chair. He struggled against his bonds for a moment, head spinning, but it was no use. He was trapped. Ellio scrunched his eyes open and closed, trying to clear his vision. Where was he? Was this a stadium?

Retiarius arena!

"Decided to join us, gutter rat?" a raspy voice spoke.

Ellio blinked and tried to focus on his blurry surroundings. He was in the stands of Retiarius's famous arena. A tall, well-dressed man stood in the aisle to his right, flanked by shorter, uniformed staff. Aside from the guards posted along the walls, the arena was empty and eerily quiet.

The man took a drag on the cigar in his hand and blew the smoke in Ellio's face.

I know him from somewhere.

Ellio's thoughts raced, trying to remember. His head throbbed.

The man leaned over him, and Ellio saw veins bulging at his temples. Bloodshot eyes glared down at him.

"I'm about to teach you some manners, *boy*. Breaking into my house. Damaging my tower. Trashing my security system." The man's voice rose in volume. "Did you honestly think you could steal from *me*? In *my* city! In my own house!" He was screaming now, saliva spraying from his lips.

"You—" Ellio started.

The man backhanded him across the face. "Don't interrupt your betters."

Then Ellio recognized him. Guild boss Tarak. He always made an appearance at the end of Retiarius matches.

Ellio tasted blood. He glared at Tarak and the guild boss laughed.

"We'll decide your fate with a special match. Our undefeated champion, Silent Nyte, will face off against her three biggest competitors: Stiletto and the Twins. If our dark angel can defeat the odds stacked against her, I'll spare your life. You'll be sold to the quarries of Gehenna to work off your debt to me under Lucien's watchful eye. If Silent Nyte loses, however, you won't leave this arena alive." Tarak flicked the ash from the end of his cigar.

Ellio swallowed. Hard.

He could see Kaya standing in the center of the arena, all in black. Her back was to him, hands clenched at her sides. She whirled around, a familiar black horned mask covering her face.

Silent Nyte!

He'd almost forgotten. Why had it taken him so long to realize? Kaya was Silent Nyte. And instead of rescuing her, he'd only made things worse.

Ellio yanked his arms against the cords but couldn't break free. Twisting his shoulders, he tried to wrench himself up at an angle. Useless. His ankles and wrists were tightly bound to the stadium chair. "Kaya! Don't worry about me. Get out of here!" he shouted.

"Quiet, boy, or I'll kill you right now," Tarak seethed.

Ellio clamped his mouth shut and glared at the guild boss. Kaya was still a valuable resource to Retiarius. But him? His life was worth nothing to the guild. If anything, he was a liability to Kaya. A cold trickle of sweat ran down his back.

Tarak crossed his arms over his chest, a satisfied glint in his eye. "Begin the match." At a wave of his hand, a gong rang out and Kaya's opponents entered the arena. Stiletto was in the lead, flanked by the Twins, Lorelai and Drynn.

Stiletto snapped her whip with relish, tossing her brown curls over her shoulder. "I've been waiting for this day," she crowed.

"You've been waiting to *lose*?" Kaya scoffed, extending her staff.

Stiletto's grin faltered. She nodded to the twins, and the three fighters charged at Kaya, who ran forward to meet them. Just before they collided, Kaya dug her staff into the ground, vaulted over them, and struck from behind. The staff swept Lorelai off her feet.

Stiletto lashed out with her whip, but Kaya launched into a back handspring.

Twirling her staff, Kaya smirked at the trio. "Is that all you've got?"

Drynn roared and charged with her trident. Lorelai threw her net. The three stalked her across the sand. Kaya deflected the net with her staff and leapt nimbly out of Stiletto's reach. Drynn thrust the trident forward, catching Kaya's staff between the prongs. For a moment the two weapons were locked. Then Kaya shifted her shoulder. The wooden staff rolled free of the trident's grip, and she jumped back.

For all their skill, the three opponents were clearly outmatched. Kaya spun her staff and motioned for them to come with a flick of her wrist.

Ellio couldn't resist a smile. *Silent Nyte at her best.*

Lorelai, Drynn, and Stiletto charged toward her. Kaya spread her feet apart in an open stance.

Tarak grunted and Ellio saw him press a button on his control panel, activating the collar's shock system.

Kaya went down on her knees with a scream. Electricity crackled over her body, leaving her gasping for breath.

"That's cheating!" Ellio cried out.

"Boy, did you think I'd make a bet I wasn't guaranteed to win?" Tarak raised a condescending eyebrow.

Ellio gritted his teeth, digging his fingers into the armrests. That's when he noticed. The bindings on his right arm were a little loose. He started twisting his hand discreetly. Pain flared up his wrist as the cords bit into his skin, but Ellio didn't stop.

Kaya was still trembling from the shock collar. Her staff fell from her hands.

Drynn kicked it away to the far wall. She lunged forward with her trident and nicked Kaya in the side.

Kaya rolled away and pressed a hand to her waist; her palm came back red with blood.

Without her staff, the other fighters moved into close range. Stiletto, Drynn, and Lorelai still had their weapons. With Kaya's reduced defense, they were able to make better use of them. Stiletto's whip caught her around the arm, restricting her movement. Drynn got a solid blow to her gut. Kaya stumbled and Lorelai was able to grab her right leg in the net and pull, dragging Kaya off her feet. Her fingers scrabbled over the sand floor trying to find some purchase, but Stiletto and Drynn were on her in an instant.

The pair hauled her back onto her knees and restrained her arms.

"You're left-handed, aren't you?" Drynn asked.

Stiletto grinned.

Drynn looped her arm around Kaya's left elbow and jerked Kaya's wrist behind her back.

Ellio could hear the pop from his seat.

Kaya screamed.

"Stop, please!" Ellio pleaded.

Stiletto shrieked with laughter. "So much for being *Silent* Nyte."

"What's the matter? Is that all you've got?" Drynn mocked, digging her hand into Kaya's shoulder.

Ellio could see Kaya writhe in Drynn's grip. His knuckles turned white on the armrest.

But then Kaya wrenched her right arm free. She curled her hand into a fist and smashed Drynn with a devastating uppercut. The twin went sailing across the sand.

Lorelai surged forward. "I'm going to carve that mask off your face!" she screeched, leaping at Kaya with a scream.

As Lorelai approached, Kaya lurched forward, head-butting her under the chin. Lorelai's head snapped back, and she fell to the ground, stunned. Blood gushed from her nose.

Kaya's mask had suffered damage as well. A chunk of the face had chipped away. One violet eye peered through the cracked demon visage.

Stiletto berated the other two girls, who scrambled to their feet and joined her.

Kaya stood on shaky legs. Her left arm hung limp at her side, right hand clutching her shoulder.

Stiletto lashed out with her whip, wrapping it around Kaya's torso, pinning her arms to her sides. Kaya let out a grunt of pain as Stiletto pulled her closer.

"I've always hated you," Stiletto whispered, so close Kaya could smell rancid moj fish on her breath.

Kaya tried to shrug, but pain shot up her arm. She forced herself to smile. "I have that effect on people."

Stiletto's eyes blazed. "I don't care if Tarak wants to keep you as his little pet. I'm going to finish what I started at the gala."

"So, it was you. What was it, poison in the sweet rolls?"

"In your drink," Stiletto hissed. "You should've died that night. I was waiting for them to find you the next day, covered in a blistering rash, body contorted in agony."

Kaya chuckled. "You must've been so disappointed."

"I like a challenge." Stiletto pulled a slender dagger from her sleeve and twirled it on her finger. "You won't be able to magic your way out of this one, Kaya." Grinning wickedly, she thrust it straight toward Kaya's heart.

Time seemed to slow. The glittering blade inched closer to her chest.

Kaya's eyes fixed on Ellio in the stands. He was shouting something, the muscles straining in his neck.

Ringing filled her ears. Darkness rimmed her vision and her lungs pinched shut. The dagger crept inexorably forward. She couldn't stop it. There was no time.

Static devoured her mind.

I'm sorry, Ellio.

"Kaya!" Her mother grabbed her hand and thrust her into the tent.

"Mama, what's happening?" Kaya cried.

"Hush, my love." Mama brushed her fingers through Kaya's hair. "I need you to stay inside the tent. No matter what happens. Understand?"

"But, Mama—"

Her mother took her daughter's face in her hands and stared into Kaya's eyes. The laugh lines around her mouth pulled down into a frown. "It's not safe. They've found us. Stay inside until I tell you to come out."

"Yes, Mama."

"That's my girl." Mama kissed her forehead and slipped from the tent.

Outside people were screaming. Kaya could hear grown-up voices. And then a great big crash. When she couldn't stand it any longer, Kaya crept forward and peeked through a seam in the tent.

Blue flames were flowing down Mama's arms. The fire made Kaya draw back from the curtain.

Fire!

Kaya paced. Fire hurt. Was Mama in pain? But her mother had looked strong, fierce. She was fighting those men. So many, Kaya couldn't count

them all. They were dressed in gray like twilight. Surrounding
Mama, throwing weapons at her, trying to knock her down. But
Mama wasn't letting them close.

Kaya's mind reeled as long-forgotten memories flooded her mind.
Her mother was a warrior. But everything had changed in an instant.

The day she'd met Dragul. The day her life was shattered. The day
she became an orphan.

Dragul!

He was there. After the attack.

Kaya could remember him now. As a child, when she had finally
dared to peel back the canvas of the tent. When all the noise had
stopped except for a low keening.

Dragul knelt on the ground. Mama was cradled in his arms, blood
trickling from her mouth. Her eyes looked like glass. Kaya remembered Dragul mumbling, "My child, my precious, precious child."

How could I have forgotten?

Kaya's thoughts raced. He was talking about Mama. She was his
daughter. He was coming to visit.

Mama was his daughter. That makes me...

Why didn't Dragul ever say anything?

The memories tumbled through her mind. His words. When he
was angry, Dragul would chide, "Kaya, your mother wouldn't be
happy." But when he was pleased, he'd praise her. "Kaya, you do your
family proud."

The hints were always there. She was just too buried in anger and
pain to recognize them.

"Kaya," Mama's voice swam through the air around her. "Never forget, we only fight when we have something to protect. But when we do, we fight to win."

Blue flames kindled in Kaya's eyes; her mother's words echoing in her mind.

I will protect Ellio.

She took a deep breath and clenched her fists, surprised to find that her arm no longer hurt. A tingling sensation crawled over her skin, like an electric charge.

Stiletto's knife was still moving toward her in slow motion.

Kaya screamed. The power building inside her blasted outward, shattering her mask and shredding apart the whip wrapped around her torso. Stiletto and the Twins were thrown backward by the force of the wind.

In the stands, Ellio saw Tarak reach for his control panel. Ellio ripped his right hand free of the restraints. Ignoring the blood dripping from his wrist, he toggled the controls of his watch, syncing it to the control panel's frequency. Tarak's device fizzled and sparked. The screen turned black with a pop.

"Now, Kaya!" Ellio shouted.

He watched Kaya, eyes blazing with blue fire, reach up and tear the collar off her throat. Ellio let out a breath he didn't realize he'd been holding.

"You filthy gutter rat!" Tarak sprang at Ellio, wrapping thick fingers around his throat. "You've interfered for the last time!"

Ellio tried to push him away with his free arm, but Tarak was like a wild animal, foamy saliva gathering at the corners of his mouth.

"Uh, Boss..." one of the guards interrupted.

"Not now!"

"Boss, you *need* to see this."

Tarak turned and backhanded the guard before the spectacle in the arena caught his eye. Blue flames spread down Kaya's arms, dripping off her fingertips like water.

Stiletto was back on her feet, wiping the blood from her mouth with a fist. "I'm not scared of you and your little light show, Kaya!" she screeched.

Kaya turned to face her, eyes glowing blue-white. "You should be."

Drynn and Lorelai howled and rushed at Kaya together. Drynn thrust her trident out. Kaya ducked, used her hands as leverage, and did a spinning roundhouse kick that sent Drynn sprawling. Lorelai threw her net. Kaya caught it with one hand. Flames ran down her arm and greedily consumed the material. Kaya opened her hand and a pile of ash slid from her palm.

Lorelai gaped at her. When Kaya took a step toward her, she stumbled and fell over. Lorelai scuttled away on her hands and knees.

With a snarl, Stiletto leapt at Kaya.

Kaya spun around, seized her wrist, and flung her against the side wall.

Stiletto slumped into a heap, curly hair plumed over her face.

Kaya turned her burning gaze toward Ellio and Tarak in the stands.

Tarak made a sweeping signal with his hand. "Get her!" he bellowed.

The security guards stationed around the arena rushed forward, climbed over the walls, and dropped into the fighting pit. With their black suits, gloves, and gleaming combat visors, it looked like a wave of darkness pouring onto the sand.

Kaya walked to her staff and flipped it into her hand with her foot. She gave it an experimental twirl as the guards surged toward her.

Spinning, dodging, striking. Kaya parried blows and knocked the guild members out with her staff until no one was left. Guards were sprawled across the arena wall or piled on the floor in groaning clumps.

Tarak reached for Ellio's throat. Kaya hefted her staff like a javelin and threw it. The staff lodged in the chair next to Ellio, an inch from Tarak's nose.

"You little fool!" Tarak roared. He yanked out Kaya's staff and broke it over his knee like a matchstick. Tossing the pieces away, he turned toward Kaya with open arms. "Money. Power. There's nothing I couldn't give you. But you've ruined everything. Awakening Eirenian powers. And for what? A filthy gutter rat."

A vein throbbed in Tarak's forehead and he rolled his shoulders. "Now I have to kill you, little bird." His lips curled into a grotesque smile, and he gnashed his teeth. "Lucien's orders are very clear. Wipe out every last Eirenian."

Dark-purple flames crept down Tarak's shoulders. He flexed his right arm as fire traced between his fingertips.

Ellio's stomach churned as he watched the shadowy flames lick across Tarak's chest. Nausea seared his throat. He fought to swallow back the burning sensation. There was something wrong with those flames. Something in their sinister glow that drove icy nails through his heart. Every nerve in his body crackled with a single message:

Run!

But he couldn't leave Kaya.

Using his free hand, Ellio yanked the cords off his left wrist, then untied his legs. He finished just in time to see Kaya vault over the arena wall and charge toward the guild boss.

She rocketed toward him, trailing blue fire, almost faster than Ellio's eyes could follow. She swung a fist at Tarak, strong enough to knock out an elephant.

But Tarak dodged.

Kaya raced toward Tarak again. She swept her right leg up in a beautiful roundhouse kick.

The guild boss knocked her foot aside with his forearm and slammed a fist into her gut. Kaya went sailing, carving a trail of destruction through the arena seats.

Ellio clenched his teeth. Tarak was a monster. He was faster and stronger than Kaya. She threw herself at him and he knocked her away, like a cat batting away a mouse.

He was toying with her.

Ellio searched his pockets. Dral! They'd taken all his tools, his utility belt. All he had left was his watch and... he patted the hidden pocket on his right boot. At least *that* was still there.

The air suddenly grew quiet. Ellio jerked his head up to see the whirlwind of fist strikes had ended. Tarak had Kaya by the throat, suspending her in the air. Kaya clawed at his fingers, but it was as if his fist were made of iron.

Ellio panicked. He had no tools left. Taking a step forward, his foot bumped against something.

Silent Nyte's staff!

Tarak shook Kaya like a rag doll. "Why do you keep fighting? It's useless. What could one little girl do all alone?"

"She's not alone!" Ellio shouted, stabbing the broken end of Kaya's staff into Tarak's leg. He jammed his thumb on the extension button and the splintered edge shot forward, skewering Tarak's calf.

The guild boss screamed and dropped Kaya. She landed in a heap on the rubble.

Ellio dodged around Tarak's howling form, grabbed Kaya, and darted behind a block of concrete that had been uprooted in the battle.

He peeked around the slab to see if Tarak was following him. The guild boss grabbed the staff and ripped it out of his leg with a roar. Blood gushed from the wound, but strangely, Tarak started laughing. The dark-purple flames swept down his leg and the blood flow dried up.

Ellio gaped. Tarak's leg was completely healed.

"Now do you understand how hopeless your situation is?" Tarak howled with laughter. "You can't win."

Ellio glanced at Kaya who was breathing heavily, eyes squeezed shut as her fingers clutched her throat. Her face and arms were nicked with cuts, and she had a large gash over her right eye.

"Kaya." Ellio took her face in his hands. "Are you all right?"

Her eyes fluttered open and fixed on his face. "Ellio." Kaya's voice was serious. "I don't think I can beat him."

"Together we can," he assured her. He swiped a thumb across her cheekbone, brushing away a smudge of dirt.

Tarak prowled the stadium, calling out, "Little bird, where are you? You can't hide forever."

Ellio cringed, dropping his hands. "He's right. We can't stay here." He shifted his feet and winced as the gravel crunched underfoot. Patting his boot, he drew a large det charge from the hidden pocket. "This should stop him."

"It looks broken." Kaya raised an eyebrow.

"It got banged up when they captured us. But once I connect the fuse..." Ellio patted his pocket. "No," he whispered desperately.

"What's wrong?"

"The fuse is *gone*. Without it, the det charge is useless." Ellio's face fell. He clenched his fists and his gaze caught on his wristwatch. With a neutrino battery. He could use that. It would certainly trigger an explosion. Even larger than the one he'd originally planned.

He looked at Kaya with a grin. "I can fix this! I just need you to buy me a few minutes."

Kaya exhaled slowly. Ellio was already fixated on the watch, analyzing how to remove the casing.

"Ellio."

The tenderness in her voice pulled him from his task and Ellio looked up as her lips brushed against his. The kiss was so soft, he thought he'd imagined it.

"Hurry!" she whispered urgently, and then she was gone, darting around the block of concrete.

Ellio stared after her a moment, a blush burning across his face, pulse drumming in his ears. He shook his head.

Focus!

Ellio lifted the glass cover off the watch to expose the inner elements. The neutrino battery was encased in an isolation cartridge. He carefully disconnected the wires and lifted out the battery. Smoke rose from the battery cell with a hiss. Neutrino batteries were powerful. Without the cartridge to stabilize it, the materials inside would begin deteriorating immediately. If Kaya threw the battery near Tarak, the force of the fall should be enough to crack open the neutrino and detonate the blast. Fumes were already leaking from the metal seam.

Ellio straightened the wires on the det charge and rigged the neutrino battery to it. The explosive hummed to life, power surging through its systems with volatile neutrino energy.

He peered over the concrete. Tarak caught Kaya's arm as she swung a fist at him and hurled her into one of the concrete support pillars. She crashed through it in a shower of rubble.

"Kaya!" Ellio raced toward her.

She stood on shaky legs, using his shoulder for support. Her nose was bleeding.

"It's ready." Ellio handed the smoking det charge to her. "How's your aim? Do you think you can throw it near him?"

Kaya smirked. "Only one way to find out." She hefted it gently, gauging its weight.

"We've only got one shot at this," Ellio warned her. "Once that thing hits the ground, KABLAM."

Kaya nodded. "Stand back."

She lobbed the det charge. It sailed through the air in a beautiful arc, heading straight for Tarak.

Kaya grabbed Ellio and the two dove behind a twisted cluster of stadium seats.

The explosion rocked the entire arena, carving great cracks through the concrete, blasting away seats and spewing a cloud of dust over everything. The ground shuddered as if they were on a boat at sea. The support pillar behind them groaned, chunks of plaster falling from the ceiling.

They got up, coughing from dust, and strained to peer through the smoke.

Then Ellio heard a sound that sent needles of terror prickling up his spine.

Laughter.

Tarak was standing in the middle of the crater, palms outstretched. Cracked concrete spread out around him in an explosive wave, but he was completely unscathed.

"You can't imagine the power Lucien's given me." He pointed a meaty fist at Kaya. "You have no idea of your own power, what you're capable of. And now you never will. You've thrown it all away."

Tarak's words burned into Ellio's skull. How was he still standing?

The stadium groaned and a few pebbles shook loose onto Ellio's head. He brushed them off, frowning. Then his gaze zipped up, and he took in the pillars around the room.

That's it!

"Kaya!" Ellio grabbed her arm and jerked his head slightly toward a pillar. Would she understand?

Kaya's eyes narrowed, and she nodded. She clenched her fists and launched herself straight at Tarak.

He laughed. "You never learn, do you?"

Kaya dropped to a slide, skidding between Tarak's legs, and slamming into the pillar behind him.

Tarak snickered. "You missed, little bird."

Kaya stood and brushed herself off. "I *don't* miss."

A deep crack split the air, fissures snaked along the pillar and crawled across the ceiling.

Tarak glanced up, just in time to see an enormous chunk of ceiling concrete slam into him from above.

From across the room, Ellio breathed a sigh of relief. His plan had worked! Tarak was sealed in an impromptu sarcophagus of concrete and rebar. It was hard to believe even someone with his powers could survive the sudden crushing weight of three tons of arena roofing material.

The room rocked and more chunks of the ceiling began to fall. Kaya's blow to the pillar had destabilized the entire structure.

Now Ellio and Kaya were also at risk of getting pulverized.

Kaya limped back toward him, breathing heavily. The flames were gone from her arms, her eyes back to their beautiful dark violet. She clutched her right side. Dark circles ringed her eyes.

Guards were scrambling up the stairs and out of the giant arched doorway. Ellio wrapped his arm around Kaya's waist and tugged her toward the exit when he heard a faint cry.

"Help!"

Ellio strained his ears. With so much noise from the collapsing arena and the shouts of the guards, maybe he'd imagined it. "Kaya, did you hear that?"

She nodded. "It sounded like it came from the fighting pit."

They stumbled to the edge of the wall and looked down.

Lorelai was still in the pit. A section of wooden planks had caved in, and her sister Drynn was trapped underneath. Lorelai saw Ellio and Kaya staring down at her. "Help us, please!" she begged.

Kaya snorted.

Ellio gripped her shoulder, tight. "We can't leave them to die."

"No, I suppose not," she grumbled.

Ellio waved at Lorelai and cupped his hands to his mouth. "We're coming!" he shouted.

Kaya and Ellio skirted the wall until they found a section that had partly collapsed. Slipping down into the arena, they hurried to the twins. Between Kaya, Ellio, and Lorelai, they were able to wedge the boards up high enough for Drynn to crawl out.

She tried to stand but dropped back to the ground with a hiss. "My ankle. I can't walk on it."

Ellio took stock of Drynn's foot. He was no doctor, but the large purplish bruise and swelling didn't look good. "Come on." He gestured to Lorelai. "We can support her together."

They stood on either side of Drynn and helped her up.

Drynn slipped an arm around their shoulders and hopped forward. "I guess this'll have to do."

Kaya glanced behind them. "Where's Stiletto?"

Lorelai jerked her head to the left. "She was still lying by the wall the last time I saw her."

Kaya muttered something under her breath and clenched her fists. "You two get moving. I'll catch up." When Ellio started to protest, she held up a hand. "Drynn can't move quickly, and we don't have much time. Get moving." Her eyes softened and she flashed him a small smile. "I'll be fine. Go."

Turning her back on him, Kaya stomped across the sand. Where had that dumb brunette gotten to? Her eyes tracked across the rubble.

There.

Stiletto had pulled herself into a sitting position against the wall. Her hair was a snarled, frizzy mess and her lip was split open.

When she noticed Kaya's approach, she sneered. "What are *you* doing here?"

"Believe me, I don't like it any more than you," Kaya muttered. "So, let's just get it over with." She held out a hand, but Stiletto slapped it away.

"I don't need you."

Kaya raised an eyebrow. "Really?" She gestured around the crumbling arena. "Do you have a death wish?"

Her words were punctuated by the shriek of metal. Another support pillar had fallen, pulling down chunks of concrete and steel.

Stiletto bit her lip and looked at Kaya with watery eyes. "Why would you help me? I tried to kill you."

"Because…" Kaya paused. She wanted to say, "Because Ellio made me," but that wasn't right. He hadn't asked her to look for Stiletto. Why *did* she come?

Then it hit her.

"I guess it's because, deep down, you and I aren't that different." Stiletto started to scoff, but Kaya cut her off. "Deep, deep down. Because on the surface, you're a twit."

Stiletto huffed. "Figures. You can't even help someone without insulting them." She took Kaya's hand. "Don't think this makes us even."

"Wouldn't dream of it," Kaya agreed, yanking her up.

The two girls limped outside as pieces of the roof rained down around them. Stumbling through the exit, they found chaos outside. People were screaming and running in every direction. Guild members fled the collapsing arena and poured into the central courtyard.

Ellio ran up to them, sweeping Kaya into a hug. "You're all right," he breathed.

She hugged him back, tight.

Stiletto made a retching sound. "Gross. All this cuteness is making me sick."

Kaya glared at her around Ellio's elbow.

Stiletto sniffed and tossed her head. "You two better leave. It's just a matter of time before someone realizes you've escaped."

"She's right." Kaya tugged on Ellio's sleeve. "That way. There's a garage where they keep the jetbikes." Her legs shook and she was favoring her right leg when she walked.

"Come on, Kaya." Ellio bent down in front of her, and she slid onto his back with a grateful sigh.

"Thanks."

"No prob. Which way again?" Ellio asked.

"To the left."

"Got it." Ellio adjusted his arms, scooting her further up his back, and started walking. "So, about what happened in there…"

"I'm half Eirenian."

Ellio stiffened. "And you never thought to mention it?"

"I'd forgotten. Until tonight, I could barely remember anything about my parents. I still don't remember much."

That made sense. Kaya had been young when her parents were murdered. Maybe forgetting was her mind's way of protecting itself.

"But what about Tarak?" Ellio protested. He could still remember the gnawing fear in his stomach as he watched the purple flames writhe around Tarak's body. "Was he Eirenian too?"

"No." Kaya shook her head, her hair tickling Ellio's neck. "He was a tool, used to kill Eirenians."

Ellio's hands felt clammy. Kill Eirenian warriors? "Why?" he wondered aloud.

Kaya's hand clenched the back of his shirt. "I'm not sure. But I plan to find out. Tarak said that Lucien gave him his power."

"Lucien? *The* Lucien? King of Gehenna? What does he have to do with all this?"

Kaya huffed. "I wish I knew. But if we want answers, we need to get out of here first."

They'd made it to the garage. The door was thrown open, probably by a panicked guild member shortly after the explosion. A row of Retiarius jetbikes glittered under the halogen lights.

Ellio helped Kaya lean against the wall. He brushed a kiss to her forehead. "I'll be right back," he promised. Ellio popped open the control panel of the nearest bike and began hot wiring.

"You're a natural," Kaya breathed. She hissed and pressed a hand against her ribs.

Ellio blushed and ducked his head. "I finally found the right motivation."

"For crime?" Kaya quipped.

"For *living*," he corrected.

Ellio slung himself onto the bike and Kaya slid in behind him. She wrapped her right arm tight around his waist, pressing her cheek between his shoulder blades.

His stomach fluttered. It felt as if he'd drunk a gallon of fizzy soda and the bubbles were dancing along his veins.

They were going to escape Beulah.

Together.

Looking back over his shoulder, he asked, "Where to?"

Kaya smiled and leaned close to whisper in his ear. "The ocean."

EPILOGUE

ELLIO HURRIED UP THE crumbling stone steps to the top of the hill. Kaya was waiting. She leaned against the guardrail, her white sleeveless dress billowing in the wind. Her hand clutched at a floppy-brimmed sunhat, pinning it to her head against the light breeze.

"It's about time," she told him in a haughty voice. "More than thirty minutes to fix a climate regulator? I think you're starting to lose your touch."

Ellio laughed. "Don't bet on it." He sidled up next to her and bumped her shoulder with his.

Kaya turned and surveyed the landscape. They were on top of a tall grassy hill. Vineyards and farmlands stretched out before them as far as the eye could see. It was a sea of green. So different from the grime of Beulah.

"It's beautiful," Kaya murmured.

"It is," Ellio agreed. But he wasn't looking at the landscape. Ellio trailed a fingertip along her arm from her wrist to her shoulder. "You're starting to get more freckles."

Kaya grunted.

Most people considered freckles a defect. But Ellio adored them.

"Have I ever told you how much I love freckles?" He leaned over and kissed her shoulder.

Kaya chuckled as his lips met her bare skin. "Only a few thousand times."

Ellio felt her tense and looked up. "Something wrong?"

She sniffed the air. "What's that delicious smell?"

"I almost forgot!" Ellio held up a paper bag, spotted with grease stains. "Niku noms. The restaurant owner gave me a bag as a thank-you for fixing his regulator."

"Niku noms?" Kaya tilted her head and Ellio grinned.

She was adorable.

"It's a local specialty. A raw egg wrapped in mincemeat, stuffed into a roll, and then fried in oil." He reached into the bag and handed her one.

Kaya tore off the top half of the paper wrapping and scrunched it in her fist. She eyed the niku nom appreciatively.

Ellio grabbed one for himself.

"It's really good," Kaya mumbled, mouth already full.

Ellio chuckled. "I've always been impressed by your appetite."

She knocked him in the shoulder, frowning. "Is that a bad thing?"

"Not at all."

Ellio took a bite. The flaky crust was buttery and delicious. Inside, the meat was juicy, with a tang of local herbs and spices. It was a perfect complement to the savory egg, the yolk still creamy and steaming.

Kaya finished her niku nom and licked her fingers. "The next town we stop in with a teleport, remind me to drop a line to Roscoe. I promised I'd let him know how we're doing."

Ellio leaned against the guardrail, propped up on his elbows. "Who knew he had such a soft spot for fighter chicks?"

Kaya clicked her tongue and elbowed him. "He's like a grandfather, you goof." But then she went still and silent, eyes staring into the distance.

"Kaya, what is it?"

"I told you about Dragul, right?"

"The guy who raised you in the desert? After your parents..." Ellio gripped the rusty guardrail, looking down.

"I think he was... my grandfather," Kaya said hesitantly.

"What?" Ellio's brows rose to his hairline, and he turned to her with a concerned expression.

"During the fight, some of my memories came back, from my childhood." At Ellio's solemn nod, she continued, "He was in them."

Ellio let out a low whistle. "And he never told you?"

"I was so angry, so confused. And he was grieving too, I think. I wasn't ready to hear it. For ten years, it was like those memories were locked away. But he told me, when we separated, to come find him in Avathys when I was ready."

They both looked off in the distance, to the east.

"If memory serves, Avathys is a country right on the coast," Ellio said.

Kaya looked down at her hands, flexing her fingers. "I need to find out more about the warriors of Eiren—about my mother and who came after my parents."

Ellio was silent for a moment, watching her. He took her hand and threaded his fingers between hers. "Then we'll find out together."

A beautiful, genuine smile kindled across Kaya's lips. Ellio stood transfixed, drinking in the sight.

Her mouth turned up into a mischievous grin. "Ready for another adventure, Ellio?"

"One step at a time," he said, drawing her into his arms.

Kaya was strong. She was light. Like a spark that could pierce the darkness or set a forest ablaze. Ellio was still terrified of her. Terrified of the heaviness in his chest that only seemed to lift when she was near. Terrified that he might never be enough.

She'd wrenched him out of his predictable little life. Out of the safety and comfort of routine. And it terrified him how much he loved her for it.

Kaya reached up to cup his face, thumbs sweeping across his cheekbones. "Are you worried?"

He sucked in a breath and leaned his forehead against hers, closing his eyes. "Not when you're with me," he whispered.

"Where would I go?" Kaya huffed. "You're like coming home."

Ellio squinted an eye open. She was looking fixedly at a spot over his shoulder, a rosy blush painting her face. The sight made a warmth bloom in his chest. Ellio felt the fear and worry slough off him, like a snake shedding its skin.

"Home?" He brushed his lips against her forehead, tucking a strand of hair behind her ear. "I like the sound of that."

Sneak Peek

Can't get enough of Kaya and Ellio?

Their adventures continue in *Beauty from Embers*, the second book in the *Beauty from Ashes* series.

Read on for a glimpse of their upcoming sequel!

Excerpt from Beauty from Embers

Kaya slammed into the dirt.

Dragul tapped his foot in the sand after neatly evading her attack. He gave her a frustrated look. "Again."

Kaya growled. The stinking old fossil never let up. She got to her feet, hiding a wince. Her calves stiffened as she bent to brush herself off.

"Don't tell me you're tired," Dragul taunted. "I'm three times your age, and I'm still waiting for you to actually start fighting."

Kaya launched herself at him, fist swallowed in blue flame. Dragul knocked it neatly aside. "Predictable means avoidable. Weak. You're still letting your emotions control you."

Kaya roared and darted forward. She feinted a punch and crouched, swinging a leg out to trip him.

Dragul leaped nimbly backward. "Better. But still too slow."

Kaya and Dragul battled across the training grounds. In reality, Kaya was just chasing after her mentor. Dragul avoided her attacks at every turn.

"I had hoped you'd learned something in our time apart," Dragul chided. "You're still relying on your anger for strength."

Kaya panted, hands on her thighs. "My anger"—*pant*—"is"—*pant*—"my strength." She leaped at him and this time Dragul stepped into her kick. He grabbed her leg and flung her away.

Kaya faceplanted, skidding across the gravel. She spat out a clump of grass and wiped her mouth. Her fist came away bloody. "I'll get you for that, you old fossil!"

"No, you won't." Dragul crossed his arms and fixed her with an assessing stare. "At the rate you're going, you'll never lay a finger on me."

Kaya roared, blue flames dancing down both shoulders, tickling her arms, flicking out from her body in little forked tongues. Then all at once, the flames winked out and Kaya sank to her knees.

"You've exhausted yourself again." Dragul walked forward and draped a towel over her head. "Time for a break."

"I can still..." Kaya stood and wobbled.

Dragul caught her, brushing her bangs back from her forehead. "That's enough for now, Kaya. Resting is also a part of training."

Kaya shoved herself off him. "I don't see how sitting around is going to make me stronger." She stomped out of the clearing and around the back of the house where Ellio was tinkering with his jetbike.

He must have heard her angry steps across the gravel, because when she rounded the corner, he peeked his head out and pushed his goggles into his dark blue hair. "How's the training going?"

Kaya glared at him.

Ellio scratched his neck with a chuckle. "That good, huh?"

Kaya crossed her arms in front of her chest and leaned against their mud and thatch farm hut. "It's that stinking old man. Dragul says '*Don't get angry, Kaya. Don't lose your temper, Kaya.*'" She made her voice into a raspy, high-pitched imitation of old age.

Ellio smiled at her and started screwing a bolt back into place with his torque wrench. "You know," he said between clicks of the wrench, "I wouldn't completely disregard his advice." He risked a glance up, but her smoldering gaze made him duck his head back down again. "Age has its wisdom," he said with a sheepish shrug.

Kaya groaned. "Not you too."

Ellio must have finished what he was working on, because he stood up, dusted off his coveralls and stepped around the bike toward her.

Ellio joined her on the wall, bumping her shoulder. He smelled faintly of earth and engine grease, but Kaya didn't mind. "Do you regret coming?" he asked her seriously. "If you're really unhappy, we could leave."

Kaya ran a hand through her hair, dislodging dust and dirt. She probed her sore lip with the tip of her tongue. "No," she said. "I don't want to leave."

The tension in Ellio's shoulders visibly dropped and Kaya immediately felt guilty. Ellio had no family left in the world. Of course, he'd want her to reconcile with her grandfather. She ground her teeth and huffed. "I'm not leaving until I figure out how he's so dratted quick."

At Ellio's wide-eyed expression, Kaya rolled her eyes. "That geezer is one slippery fish. I couldn't even get one good strike in today."

"Or any day," Ellio teased. At her frown, he relented and rubbed her shoulder. "There's a lot you can learn from him. Try to consider things from his perspective." She opened her mouth to argue, but he spoke hastily to smother her protest. "I know it's not your style, but think of it like adapting to a new enemy." As he talked, Kaya saw he was really warming to the idea. Ellio slapped his fist on his palm. "Like he's a villain you have to defeat. But to defeat him, you need to think like him."

She raised an eyebrow. "So, Dragul's a villain now?"

Ellio gave her an exasperated look. "You know what I mean," he grumbled, toying with the knob of his torque wrench. "I don't mean Dragul's an actual villain, but you've gotta predict his next move. Anticipate his attacks and his defenses."

Kaya tapped a finger against her chin and hummed. Maybe Ellio was on to something. The old geezer was always after her to let go of her anger and be self-controlled. If she anticipated his strikes, she could find a weak spot. If she could land a blow, maybe he'd give up correcting her and let her train the way she wanted.

Kaya let out a snicker. Beat the old man at his own game. That *would* be fun. She knocked Ellio on the shoulder. "Maybe you're right, Ellio."

Share Your Voice

Thank you for reading *City of a Thousand Tears*. If you enjoyed this novella, please consider leaving a review. Reviews help readers discover new books and help authors learn more about creating stories you'll love.

Get Connected

Sign up for Pamela's newsletter to get a free short story at
pamelahartwrites.com

Instagram: @pamelahartwrites
Pinterest: @pamelahartwrites
Facebook: @pamelahartwrites

Acknowledgements

To those adventurous, meticulous readers who have journeyed with me this far, thank you. May your steps be filled with laughter, love, and wonderful stories.

To Lisa Hatfield, thank you for being an inspiration, an encourager, and a friend.

To Carrie Kneeland, thank you for always being willing to read another draft. Thank you for your patience and your good eye for grammar. No matter the distance, you always have my back.

To Krysta Maravilla, a fantastic critique partner, who inspired the epic final battle. I'm so excited for *Spark*!

To my Word Weaver pals, Susan Simpson, Kim Miller, Penny Hunt, Eva Marie Everson, and Carey Clark, words can't express my appreciation for all your honest feedback and support. I am privileged to be a part of your group.

To Joe Hart, the love of my life, thank you for all your advice on the male psyche. Thank you for talking through drafts and character sketches with me into the wee hours of the night. I love you.

To Willy and Marvin, my beloved fur babies, thank you for your unconditional love. Thank you for bringing joy to my life. I owe you lots of walks, belly rubs, and tug-o-war battles now that this book is finished.

To the one who set my heart free, Jesus Christ, my Lord and Savior. Everything I am and everything I have, I owe to you.

About the Author

Pamela is the author of *Beauty from Ashes, Beauty from Embers*, and *City of a Thousand Tears*. She grew up on a steady diet of fantasy, science fiction, and anime. She spent the majority of her childhood failing to acquire a Boston accent. Since then, she has slurped ramen in Ikebukuro, stampeded through flamenco lessons in Granada, and splashed her way across a fishpond for the Milkman Triathlon in Dexter. During her travels, she tends to overpack horrendously, but never regrets cramming her backpack full of books to devour along the way. She wanders the planet with Joe, the love of her life, Jacob, her sunshine baby, and her adorably maniacal Boston terriers, Willy and Marvin.

For information on her latest releases and more, check out pamelah artwrites.com

www.ingramcontent.com/pod-product-compliance
Lightning Source LLC
Chambersburg PA
CBHW050827180626
46814CB00004B/1498